The Highlander's Iron Will

A Highland Defender Novella

by

Amy Jarecki

Rapture Books
Copyright © 2017, Amy Jarecki
Jarecki, Amy
The Highlander's Iron Will

ISBN: 9781975752835

First Release: April, 2017 in The Forbidden Highlands boxed set
Second Edition: September, 2017

Book Cover Design by: Dar Albert
Edited by: Scott Moreland

All rights reserved. The unauthorized reproduction or distribution of this copyrighted work, in whole or part, by any electronic, mechanical, or other means, is illegal and forbidden.

This is a work of fiction. Characters, settings, names, and occurrences are a product of the author's imagination and bear no resemblance to any actual person, living or dead, places or settings, and/or occurrences. Any incidences of resemblance are purely coincidental.

To my wonderful mother who always encouraged me to reach for the stars.

Foreword

Skye of Clan Iain Abrach will always remember the day that marked the end of an era. Though the preceding fortnight brought a myriad of emotion from great joy to heinous terror, forever she will puzzle over the cold, amoral and outrageous order passed down from powerful men who had never set eyes on the awe-inspiring magnificence of the Coe.

Those men knew nothing of honor, of duty. They knew nothing of Highland hospitality or the community of clan and kin. Those men were naught but self-serving, cold-blooded murderers.

The clansmen and women who survived were changed forever. Often, Skye ponders that day while a clammy shiver courses across her skin…

Chapter One

Glencoe, 1st February, 1692

"No mistakes!" Mistress NicGilleasbuig insisted, slapping a measuring ribbon against her palm. "Tamp that row down again. 'Tisn't sitting smoothly enough."

"Yes, Mistress." Skye picked up the tapestry beater and worked it through the strands of wool for the third time. A student of the art of weaving, she'd been handpicked by the laird's wife. Though the woman was a hard taskmaster, Skye was fortunate to be learning a trade in the weaver's shop.

A mighty racket came from the courtyard with whistles and men yelling. Skye tensed as Mistress NicGilleasbuig, hastened to the window. "Something's afoot."

Skye sprang to her feet and joined the matron. A rider galloped past the weaver's cottage, jumped down from his garron pony and ran for the enormous oak door of the manse. "MacIain! Glenlyon and the redcoats are riding in from Ballachulish."

Skye drew her hand over her mouth to muffle her gasp.

"Lord save us." Mistress NicGilleasbuig clutched her heart while the look of dread stretched her stalwart features.

All work came to an abrupt halt. Even the clang from the smithy's shack stopped.

Skye had heard tale of Captain Robert Campbell, Laird of Glenlyon. Of all Clan Iain Abrach's enemies, Glenlyon, black sheep of Clan Campbell, topped the list. He and his thieving clan oft prayed on the Coe, reiving cattle and setting crofts to fire and sword. Until this day, attacks had subsided for a good two years after the great Glencoe chieftain had led a raid and swiped Glenlyon's prized stallion. When the dust settled, MacIain agreed to a truce by arranging for his youngest son to marry Glenlyon's niece.

Skye followed the matron out the door while more clansmen clambered into the courtyard. "Why on earth would the captain be leading his regiment into Glencoe of all places?"

"No good reason, I'll tell you now," said Mistress NicGilleasbuig, wringing her hands.

Though the prior sennight's snow had melted, a chilly wind blew from the northwest and Skye clutched her arisaid tight around her shoulders. Everywhere, the courtyard turned into a flurry of activity while men toting all manner of weapons from muskets to shovels, raced to defend the laird. And now the clang of the smithy's shop was replaced by urgent shouts and murmurs.

"Hide your weapons," boomed Hugh MacIain, heir to the clan seat, shoving his sword into a drift of snow. "Da signed the oath of fealty to William of Orange. Mark me, we shall not engage. They must draw first blood."

In the distance, Glenlyon rode at the head of his regiment, dressed in a red-coated uniform, just as all the men behind him did. He wore a long, curly periwig powdered gray beneath his tall grenadier hat and looked more Englishman than Highland laird. Carried on the wind, the snare of the drummers kept time with the march.

Mistress NicGilleasbuig grasped Skye by the shoulders. "You'd best go back inside. Hide in the loft. Lord only kens what Glenlyon is up to. If a battle erupts, those soldiers are capable of unthinkable acts. This is no place for a young woman, especially one as bonny as you."

"But—"

"Do it I say."

"Yes, Mistress." Skye curtseyed then hastened inside and climbed the ladder, but she wasn't about to hide behind the bolts of cloth and wool, not when so much excitement was happening down below. The most notorious Campbell in all of Scotland was paying Glencoe a visit in broad daylight. How could she resist peering out the loft window just for a glimpse at the devil's face?

Skye drew aside the curtain as Captain Campbell held up his hand, pulled on his horse's reins and stopped directly below her window. Glenlyon was flanked by a half-dozen dragoons on horseback and behind them, a great many foot soldiers. Clouds of breath swirled above the soldiers' heads while their muskets remained pointed down, their pikes still—a good sign for certain.

An officer seated on a bay garron pony and wearing a Highlander's feathered bonnet glanced up. His gaze met Skye's before she could back away from the pane. He smiled.

Skye slipped out of sight for a moment, her heart racing. Why were the soldiers here? Odd. Not only had an officer noticed her, he'd grinned. The last thing she expected was affability. Though the moment passed in a blink of the eye, his smile had been sincere, his eyes shiny, his face…Skye sighed. Indeed, his face was rather attractive.

After patting her chest and taking a few calming breaths, she dared to again move closer to the window. The smiling officer sat tall in his saddle, broad-shouldered and proud. He wore the red coat of the government, but also a kilt of hunter green and navy blue. The length of tartan came from beneath his coat, draped over his shoulder and was gallantly pinned in the Highland style as if he was quite proud of his kin. Was he a backstabbing Campbell, or did he pay fealty to some other clan? That he paid fealty to William of Orange went without question. Further, by simply donning a coat of red and riding in the company of Glenlyon spoke volumes about his character. No man wearing a government uniform, no matter how amiable his mien, could be a friend of Clan Iain Abrach.

The officer looked ahead expectantly and Skye followed his line of sight. Alasdair MacIain MacDonald, chief of the clan of Glencoe, stood on the stoop of the manse looking every bit the great laird and warrior. A man the clan loved and respected. At a mammoth six-foot seven-inches, the chieftain's long ginger beard may have turned white, but that only served to make him appear more menacing—just like the spiked moustache, the blue bonnet cockeyed over his thick white tresses pushed back enough to expose the deep scar on his right cheek. His countenance alone was enough to give anyone pause. But that, combined with his enormous stature, left no question as to who was chief of the great and fearsome clan of the Coe.

Hugh, his son, who was nearly as tall and every bit as formidable, marched forward with his chin tilted up in question while Glenlyon sent an officer to meet the MacIain heir with papers in hand—but not the Highlander who had smiled. This officer wore red breeches with black boots to his knees, his face shadowed by his tricorn hat.

Skye turned her ear to the glass to better hear the conversation taking place but paces away from her hiding place.

"Do you come as friends or as enemies?" Hugh asked.

"As friends," said the redcoat in an English accent, pushing the papers toward him. "We require quarters."

Skye's jaw dropped. Glenlyon and his men intended to stay? Before she caught herself, her gaze slipped downward.

As if he sensed her looking, Mr. Bright-eyes caught her yet again.

Pretending not to notice, Skye quickly shifted her attention to Hugh, who was nearly as menacing as his father.

"For how long?" He took the missive and read while mumbles of dissention rumbled through the gathering crowd.

"Until Captain Campbell's orders come," said the officer.

Hugh looked past the Englishman to Glenlyon, sitting a shiny and proud-looking Norfolk Trotter. "You mean to say your leader is not traveling through the Rannoch Moor path to visit his missus at Meggerine Castle?"

"Ah…" The officer glanced backward to the captain who gave a single shake of his head. "No. Colonel Hill commanded us to await his orders here in Glencoe."

Hugh rolled the papers and stashed them in his belt. "Well then, may I extend to you the hospitality of the Coe and Clan Iain Abrach. You and your men are welcome."

Again, Skye's mouth fell open. Had she heard correctly? A mob of redcoats rode into Glencoe requesting quarters and the laird's son extends the hand of Highland hospitality? It was February for heaven's sake. Where on earth would the lot of them sleep?

Stepping down from his stoop, Alasdair MacIain MacDonald, the clan chief himself, strode forward. A grin stretched wide across his face, his arms open wide, his palms turned to the heavens demonstrating a warm greeting. "Captain Robert Campbell of Glenlyon. To what do we owe this honor?"

After closing the distance on his steed, the most notorious enemy of Skye's clan dismounted. "I've come to visit my niece. She wed your son afore I had an opportunity to wish her good cheer."

MacIain grinned and shook the backstabber's hand. "I'm certain Sarah and Sandy will enjoy your company if you aim to stay for a wee bit."

"Yes, indeed. I hope our presence here will not cause you undue hardship. But these are difficult times and to impose ourselves upon you in such weather." The captain pointed his thumb northward. "'Tis most unfortunate that Fort William is full. Have you heard?"

"Nay, word hasn't yet reached us." The laird peered around Glenlyon and his officers. "How many men are in your regiment?"

"A small company—myself, my nephew, Lieutenant Kier Campbell, Lieutenant Lindsay, Sergeant Barber, Sergeant Hendrie, Corporals Campbell, MacPhail and Kennedy." As he spoke, Glenlyon gestured to each man with an upturned palm. "And I've fifty-seven foot in my ranks."

Skye again looked to Mr. Bright-eyes. *So, he is a Campbell. A Mr. Kier Campbell.*

The clan chief scratched the long whiskers on his chin, his gaze shifting to his eldest son. "Not a problem. Of course 'tis the Highland way to provide bed and comfort to a gentleman and a friend. I have a chamber above stairs I hope will meet with your approval."

"No, no. I'd rather be a wee bit closer to my niece." Glenlyon pointed. "I'll stay with MacDonald of Inverrigan at the bend of the glen. However, I'm sure Lieutenant Lindsay will be quite comfortable with your chamber."

Skye pressed her palms against the window. *Why not Kier Campbell? Will he be rooming with MacDonald of Inverrigan as well?*

The MacIain tapped his fingers to his lips, his eyes shifting across the cottages that peppered the glen. "I suppose we'll have to split the rest of the troops—two or three to a cottage? Hugh, Og," he hollered to his sons. "Go spread the word. Every cottage must house at least two soldiers, more if they have the means."

Hugh's eyes popped wide. "Truly?"

"Go on now." The big man flicked his hands at them, then turned to the captain. "I trust you're ready for your nooning. Bring your officers indoors and I'll have Cook prepare a meal to melt the frost from your beards."

Below, Lieutenant Campbell picked up his reins, but before he rode on, his gaze returned to Skye's window. He tipped his bonnet with a bow of his head—awfully polite for a redcoat.

***

"Next," said Lieutenant Kier Campbell, signaling for two dragoons to step forward. He'd been lumbered with the task of assigning the soldiers to their bunks, a duty that wasn't new to him especially in the Highlands. Forts were sparse. The army had naught but to rely on the kindness of the locals both for food and shelter.

But today's task didn't sit well with Kier. He was a Campbell after all, and his family's lands had been reived by Alasdair MacIain MacDonald and his notorious Clan Iain Abrach just over two years past. Why Colonel Hill had ordered Glenlyon's regiment to Glencoe, Kier couldn't fathom. MacIain had pledged fealty to King William and, ever since, the western Highlands had been at relative peace. Though set in their ways, the Jacobite loyalists had a way of putting clan and kin before king and country. Kier couldn't disagree with that, however. He, too, was Highland bred. In fact, as he'd watched the exchange earlier this day, he'd realized the only difference between him and Hugh MacIain was the fact that Kier had been born a son of a laird who paid fealty to Clan Campbell; and on the other side of Rannoch Moor, Hugh had been born to a laird who paid fealty to Clan

Donald. Both heirs were tall with muscular builds and were each groomed to assume the burden of clan chieftainship.

As the two soldiers saluted, the next Glencoe farmer stepped forward, his eyes dark and filled with distrust, just like all the others. Kier had grown impervious, however, and addressed the man diplomatically. "How many soldiers are you able to sleep?"

"None if it were up to me."

Kier had heard those words at least ten times before. "I'll assign you two, then."

The blighter scowled. "Bloody backstabbers."

"I trust you'll find Sentinels MacCallum and Nicoll trustworthy men. Put them to work. Not a one of us should discount your generous hospitality."

The MacIain man didn't look pleased. "Come along, ye reivers. I've wasted enough time this day."

After Kier had assigned all the soldiers to quarters, there was but one MacIain man remaining who had yet to take in borders. Kier held out his gloved hand. "I'm Lieutenant Campbell, sir."

"Jimmy MacDonald here." The man glowered at Kier's hand and opted not to shake it.

Splaying his fingers, Kier glanced around to see if he may have missed another, more accommodating clansman. Unfortunately, they were the only two left standing in the chieftain's courtyard. "It appears I've nay choice but to billet myself with you."

"Aye, that would be right. But make no bones about it, you'll be earning your keep if ye darken my door."

Kier offered a reluctant bow. "I'd expect no less, sir."

Jimmy looked Kier from head to toe. "Well, follow me, then. But I'll not be granting any special accommodations just 'cause you're an officer. And by the size of you, ye ought to be good for some heavy lifting."

Kier gestured for the man to lead onward. "Of course, sir."

"We live simple lives. Not a one of us puts on airs."

"Good to hear, sir."

Jimmy harrumphed and continued on his way until they arrived at a stone cottage with a thatched roof not far from Alasdair's manse.

"Are you kin with the chief?" Kier asked.

"Aye, second cousin." Jimmy opened the door. "'Tis why we enjoy luxuries such as a cast-iron hob for cooking."

Many of Kier's tenants on the other side of Rannoch Moor would be proud of a hob as well. Some lived in shielings with but a fire pit over which to cook their meals. He ducked his head below the lintel, stepped inside, removed his musket from his shoulder and set it beside the door as a gentleman ought.

"Sineag," Jimmy barked, sounding like a curmudgeon in a foul mood. "We've another mouth to feed for Lord kens how long."

Kier's gaze swept to the woman standing beside the hearth, but quickly passed her by. Any red-blooded man would be helpless not to shift his stare a wee bit further. His breath caught when he met the lass's striking blue eyes for the third time that day. Removing his bonnet, he couldn't help his grin. Devil's fire, she was bonny with mahogany hair that shone in the lamplight and an oval face like a doll with round doe-eyes.

Jimmy slapped him on the back. "Well, do not just stand there, come in and meet the family." He introduced Kier, then gestured across the room. "My wife, Sineag, my daughter, Miss Skye, and in the corner is the youngest, Tommy."

"Pleased to make your acquaintance." Kier bowed. "I trust I'll not be too much of a burden."

Everyone stared. Tommy dashed across the dirt floor and stood in front of his mother with his arms crossed and his eyebrows drawn together in a hostile expression. It was like a standoff. MacIain against Campbell, Jacobite against the government and there Kier stood with orders not to cause a stir. He scraped his teeth over his bottom lip as his gaze shifted back to the lass.

She glanced between her parents before a nervous giggle played on her lips. "Only one dragoon, Da?"

"The lieutenant was the last."

Skye moved forward and nodded to a bench at the table. "Please have a seat whilst we finish preparing the evening meal." She was much smaller than she'd appeared from the upstairs window of the weaver's shop.

Kier bowed. "My thanks."

She gave her brother's mop of brown locks a tussle. "Come, Tommy. It looks as if he's not planning to bite anyone."

The lad lowered his hands and continued to stare, his expression growing curious.

Jimmy took a seat in a wooden chair across the room. It was a typical cottage with hearth and hob on one end and a box bed on the other. In the middle stood a rectangular table, and along the walls were shelves stacked with dishes and cookware. Nearer the bed were two large trunks, used to stow clothing, no doubt.

"How long do you reckon the regiment will be in Glencoe?" asked Mistress Sineag.

Kier stretched his legs under the table and crossed his ankles. "Not long, I hope. We're to wait for the colonel's orders."

Jimmy filled his clay pipe with tobacco. "But why here? Why not in Appin or at Dunollie with the MacDougalls?"

Kier shrugged. "I'm merely an officer of the crown. My place is not to ask why. But if I'd ventured to guess, I reckon it's on account of Glenlyon's niece."

"I kent that marriage would lead to no good," said Jimmy, lighting his pipe with a twig from the fire.

Kier kept his mouth shut, but had to agree. He'd grown up with Sarah Campbell and she'd always been a bit of a shrew. It hadn't surprised him when her father arranged the marriage to Sandy. It was a way of making a truce with an untrustworthy adversary without paying too high a price.

Tommy wandered over and sat beside Kier. "What do you do for the army?"

"I'm the lieutenant in charge of the regiment's musketeers, among other things."

The lad pointed to Kier's musket. "Are you a good shot?"

"Good enough for the army." In truth, Kier was a sharpshooter, but there was no point in boasting about it.

"Would you teach me how to shoot?" the lad asked.

"Tommy, you mustn't burden our guest," scolded his mother.

Jimmy blew smoke out his nose. "I don't reckon the lieutenant will be around long enough to give lessons to ten-year-old lads, not when he has a regiment of men to train."

Kier gave the boy a wink. "If there's time and your parents approve, I'd be happy to give you a wee lesson."

The lad grinned. At least Kier had won over one of his hosts.

Miss Skye placed a spoon in front of him. "Are you fond of lamb stew, Mr. Campbell?"

"I am." Kier inhaled the scent of rose. It was the midst of winter. How did the lass manage to smell of roses rather than wood smoke and peat?

He watched as she prepared the table with bread and bowls filled to the brim with stew. After her parents took their places, Skye sat across the table from Kier. He reached for his spoon but quickly drew his hand away when Mistress Sineag cleared her throat. "We shall pray."

Tommy grabbed Kier's right hand while Miss Skye reached over and offered her palm. He took it with a grin. His heart fluttered when she smiled back. But then she shuttered her eyes as Jimmy commenced the prayer. If Kier had been quizzed on what had been said, he would have failed miserably. He was transfixed and focused on the beauty seated before him with her hand in his—petite, warm, soft and as delicate as a bird.

"Amen," Jimmy said, echoed by the others.

Miss Skye raised her long lashes and met Kier's gaze. A bit of mischief flickered in those luminous eyes while her tongue slipped to the corner of her mouth. "Ah..." she tugged her hand away.

Kier cleared his throat. "Pardon me. Amen."

"Do you not pray, Lieutenant?" asked Mistress Sineag.

"I am fond of praying, Matron. I must admit, my tongue twisted for a moment. As an army man, it is not oft I have the pleasure of dining with such a bonny maid as Miss Skye."

"You'd best not grow accustomed to it," said Jimmy with a glower. "My daughter is working in the weaver's shop until she marries."

Kier dabbed his lips with his fingers. "Are you promised, Miss Skye?"

The lass blushed clear up to her hairline.

Mistress Sineag shoveled a scoop of stew with her spoon. "She's too particular, this one. If she's not careful, she'll end up a spinster."

With a wave if his hand, Kier batted away the mother's concern. "Surely there are many years yet to come afore such a moniker is pinned on one so bonny."

A flash of anger flashed through Miss Skye's expressive blues. "Why is it my marriage prospects always command the conversation at the evening meal? I'm but nineteen years of age and I've only rejected one suitor—the hapless drunkard. Heavens, with Glenlyon riding into Glencoe this very day, there are far more interesting topics." She picked up her cup of ale, her hand trembling. "Tommy, I saw you playing shinty with the lads in the courtyard. How did your side fare?"

Kier reached for his ale as well. Picking it up, he gave the lass a nod in silent toast. Miss Skye had gumption for certain. He liked a woman would could speak for herself. He liked it a great deal.

Chapter Two

As she lay atop the box bed, Skye listened to the heavy breathing as it echoed throughout the cottage. Her parents were shut in below where they always slept, but she'd exchanged places with Tommy. By the light from the fire, she could make out the lad's wee form slumbering on her pallet near the hearth. Across from him lay Kier Campbell, the lieutenant. It was strange having a Campbell sleeping right there in the cottage. Further, the man slept on his side as if he hadn't a care. As if it were perfectly normal for him to be there.

Nonetheless, Da had gone to bed with a dirk in his hand. This night, all the folk in Glencoe were sleeping with one eye open, even though the laird had reassured them that nary a soul would accept Highland hospitality and turn backstabber. Not even a Campbell.

Skye rolled to her back and pushed the heels of her hands into her temples. Their uninvited guest was inexplicably unnerving. True, his manners were impeccable, but all evening he'd stared at her with those midnight eyes. They were curiously dark, not to mention intense and shiny and…well, they made her so…so…*befuddled*.

Neither did it help matters that the man might just be the brawest creature she'd ever seen. Tall, masculine, with a square jaw and an intelligent brow. He wore his dark tresses pulled back with a ribbon, but by the end of the evening meal, a thick lock had sprung free and hung in a lazy wave along his cheek. It was all Skye could do not to reach out and touch the hair to see if it felt as silky as it looked.

Groaning, she let out a long breath. In winter, the sun was always late to rise and Skye had been lying awake for an eternity already. She might as well climb down from the bed and set to her chores. With a lantern, she could manage the washing just as well now as she could in daylight.

Her mind made up, she crept down the ladder trying not to make a sound...until a timber groaned beneath her foot. Holding her breath, she froze in place. The Highlander across the cottage didn't move. There was no sound of her parents stirring either. To avoid the risk of another loud creak, Skye hopped down, donned her boots and pulled an arisaid around her shoulders. After tiptoeing to the hearth, she quickly lit an oil lamp, then picked up the washing and darted out the door to the River Coe which cut through the back of their lands. Night had brought on a heavy frost and her nose ran. Skye hastened her step to warm herself, knowing full well the water would be icy and miserable. At least the river ran fast enough and rarely froze solid.

Shivering, she set the basket down at the river's edge and crouched beside it. The idea of dipping her fingers in the chilly water always made her shudder to her toes but the washing had to be done. And the faster she worked, the sooner she'd be back in the warm cottage. She picked up the cake of soap and went to work.

"Do you always start your chores afore ye break your fast?"

Skye startled at the deep voice behind her. Snapping her head around, she gasped. Something had told her it was the lieutenant, but he'd taken her by surprise all the same. "Ah...I couldn't sleep."

He took a seat on the rock beside her and smiled casually as if they'd been friends for years. "Neither could I, though I must say, 'tis not the best of ideas for a maid to venture out alone afore the sun rises."

Returning to her work, Skye scraped her teeth over her bottom lip. After Glenlyon promised he'd come on friendly terms, she hadn't worried about her personal safety. "Are you saying your men are not to be trusted?"

"Nay, lass. I'm saying a woman as bonny as you shouldn't be out in the dark alone."

Her insides fluttered as if she'd never heard a compliment before. What was it about the lieutenant that made her so self-aware? "The folks in these parts are my kin. Nary a one would lift a finger to harm me." She twisted the wet linen to wring out the water, her fingers freezing to the bone.

"Allow me." A warm palm covered her hand as Mr. Campbell pulled the cloth away.

Skye thought to stop him, but when she met his gaze, the determination in his eyes gave her pause. "I reckon a man like you has never had to do the washing."

He twisted the fabric making twice as much water cascade to the river. "I reckon you are correct, miss."

She rocked back on her haunches and studied him. "What is your relation to Glenlyon?"

"He's my uncle."

"Then you were born to a life a privilege?" she asked.

"Of sorts, I suppose."

Trying not to appear too interested, Skye reached for the next piece of bed linen and dunked it in the river. "Does your family live in a castle?"

He tossed his cloth into the basket. "Aye—Sigurd Castle on Loch Dochart."

"Oh, my. I cannot even imagine what it would be like."

"Draughty on a day as chilly as this."

"Are you a second son, then?"

"Nay, the only son. I have four elder sisters."

"I beg your pardon." Skye stopped with her hands in the water. "You're the heir of a castle and you joined the army? Why ever would you do that?"

"My father thought it would turn me into a man."

"I see." She furiously worked up a lather. "And has it?"

"Turned me into a man?"

"Aye."

"I reckon so. Besides, my da pays fealty to Glenlyon. My service is expected."

"That is unfortunate." She twisted the linen.

Mr. Campbell chuckled as he again plucked it from her fingers.

"Do you think I'm humorous?" she asked.

"I think you're quite perceptive. Many a man has wondered the same. Unfortunately, my uncle's philandering ways have given him an unsavory reputation that will follow the man the rest of his days."

"But you do not condone his habits?"

"I may be my uncle's man, but I have my own opinions."

"Interesting." She reached for another piece, a shirt this time.

Mr. Campbell held the damp bed linen to his nose. "Mm. That's why you smell like roses."

Though Skye was half-frozen, heat spread through her cheeks. "Ma uses rose petals in the lye."

He gave it another sniff before tossing it in the basket. "'Tis nice."

Skye hurried to wash the remaining clothes while Mr. Campbell stayed right beside her and wrung out every piece. When she was done, she stood and blew on her freezing hands.

"Allow me to warm them." The lieutenant took her fingers between his palms and gently rubbed—rough hands, warm, welcoming. He didn't act like a Campbell in the slightest. "We'd best take you indoors afore your hands freeze solid."

No matter how wonderfully fantastic Mr. Campbell's palms felt, she tugged her hands away and crossed her arms. "I'll be fine. I've done the washing in winter many times afore."

His eyes reflected kindness, yet they were still darker than sin. "You are a resilient maid. I reckon not one of my sisters would have been able to wash a single apron in that frigid water."

"I would expect not for ladies born to privilege. Tell me, is your da a laird?"

"A lesser laird, much like Alasdair MacIain is to Clan Donald."

Skye waggled her eyebrows. "I'd wager your da's not as fearsome as our clan chief, though."

"Aye, not a man in the Highlands matches MacIain's notorious reputation. Though my da is a commanding presence in his own right."

Skye stooped to pick up the basket. "Much like his son, is he?"

Mr. Campbell took the washing from her grasp and easily balanced it on his hip. "I think not. My father is nowhere near as affable as I."

***

By the time they returned to the cottage, everyone was awake. Jimmy plastered on a scowl and faced Kier with his fists on his hips. "Where have the pair of you been at his hour?"

"Mr. Campbell helped me with the washing." Skye pointed to the hearth. "You can put the basket over there."

"The lieutenant?" asked Mistress Sineag, disbelief filling her voice.

"Aye, ma'am. I didn't reckon the lass should be out alone afore daylight." Kier set the basket down and looked to the rafters. "Shall I hang these for you?"

"Women's work," Jimmy growled.

"Thank you." Mistress Sineag gave her husband a thump on his shoulder. "Skye, set the table, please. The porridge is ready."

By the time the morning meal was served, Kier had the washing draped over the rafters. It baffled him how Jimmy discounted the task as women's work. Skye and her mother were both too short to reach. They would have needed to climb up on a stool.

"Do you think you'll have time to teach me to shoot today?" asked Tommy.

"Not certain of my orders, but if time allows, I'll be sure to find you." Kier looked to Jimmy. "Are you not a musketeer, sir?"

Jimmy frowned with a sniff. "A bow and arrow serves me just fine."

Kier returned his attention to this porridge. Muskets were expensive and many a man couldn't afford one. Even in Glenlyon's regiment half the foot were pikemen. Kier should be more conscious of MacDonald's circumstances in the future. He'd most likely insulted his host.

A knock came at the door. "Lieutenant, the captain wants a word afore muster."

Kier recognized the voice as belonging to Sentinel Nicoll. After taking one more bite, he stood. "With luck, we'll see our marching orders and I'll no longer be a burden to you kind folk."

Mistress Sineag smiled and smoothed her hand over her coif, but Jimmy snarled. "I'd be happy to see your backside marching out of the Coe for certain."

"Da!" Skye cringed, looking mortified. Perhaps Kier had earned a bit of favor with the lass by helping with the washing? If only their circumstances were different, he might enjoy courting such a lass.

He retrieved his musket and shoved his feathered bonnet atop his head, then followed the sentinel a half-mile away to the Inverrigan farm. Glenlyon had set up a makeshift office near the hearth in Brody MacDonald's cottage. "What took you so long?"

"Helped with a few chores." Kier moved to the table and sat beside Lieutenant Richard Lindsay.

"Forever the bloody Good Samaritan," said Glenlyon.

Lindsay sniggered, the bloody Sassenach. "He'll have them all eating out of his palm before our orders come."

"Wheesht." Kier reached for a scone and took a bite. Thanks to Glenlyon, he hadn't had time to finish his porridge. "I was hoping we'd be moving out today."

"Not likely," said the captain. "You'd best find a peg on which to hang your bonnet. We'll be settling in for a good while."

"Wonderful."

"Don't tell me you haven't charmed your host." Glenlyon winked at Lindsay. "Good God, Campbell, you've had an entire night."

Snorting, Kier shrugged. "I doubt my host will ever warm to me. Every time I take a gander in the direction of his daughter, he looks as if he's about to blow steam out his ears."

"She's pretty, is she?" asked Lindsay.

Kier balled his fist. "She's—"

"Not for either of you." Glenlyon shook a gnarled finger directly at Kier as if he'd made a grave misstep. "Leave the lassie alone and mind your orders."

"That's exactly what I aim to do, sir." Kier glanced between the two officers. "Pray tell, what *are* my orders?"

"Keep the men busy and out of trouble. March them from dawn to dusk."

Kier rolled his eyes. Marching, the endless grind of a soldier's typical day when there was nothing else to occupy his time. "Marching it is, sir."

"Nothing else, sir?" asked Lindsay.

"One more thing." Glenlyon leaned in and lowered his voice. "Keep this under wraps, but I want to know if any Jacobite sentiment comes out. Anything at all."

"Didn't MacIain sign the oath of fealty to the king?" asked Kier.

"He did, but two days late."

Everyone knew MacIain wasn't to blame for his tardiness. Kier held up a finger. "Because of weather."

Glenlyon shook his head. "That's a moot point."

"But there are others who have yet to come forward," said Lindsay.

"That also is not my concern. If I can prove MacIain to be a backstabbing Jacobite, I'll put him and his reiving clan under fire and sword this very day."

With a sickening twist of his gut, Kier leaned back, knitting his brows. "These are but families."

"Families who breed treasonous barbarians," said Lindsay.

Kier stood, giving his cohort a frown. "Thus far, they've done nothing but show us Highland hospitality. It is our duty to respond graciously and show them the good nature of the king's men."

"Aye," said Glenlyon. "Until they try to slit our bloody throats."

Chapter Three

Invited to a clan gathering, the soldiers congregated on the north side of the bonfire, looking on like a mob of uncomfortable and out of place dragoons. On the other side of the fire, families huddled close together. They, too, appeared a wee bit on edge. For a gathering, there weren't many smiles. Laughter was every bit as sparse as well.

Kier stood beside Lieutenant Lindsay with a tankard of ale in his hand. "It's a balmy eve for February."

The officer harrumphed. "The calm before the storm, I say."

"I say MacIain is born with a silver spoon. A sennight ago, no one would have been able to find a dry stick of wood for a fire, let alone sit out in a blizzard for a gathering." Kier took a long pull on his frothy beer. Lindsay was right about the weather to come, of course, not that it was overly warm. It just wasn't freezing at the moment.

"I wish the young fellas would turn the spit faster. My stomach's growling," said Nicoll.

"Your stomach's always bloody growling." Kier gestured toward the lads with his tankard. "Why not offer to give them a hand? Tommy looks like he could use a spell."

Nicoll snorted. "I beg your pardon? I thought we were the guests."

"We're the bloody uninvited interlopers." Kier flicked his fingers toward the spit. "Go on. Nicoll and Robertson, relieve the lads."

"You're soft," Lindsay mumbled.

Kier gripped the ear of his tankard a bit tighter. "Where the hell did that come from? Look at us. We're enjoying the hospitality of the MacIains and the lot of you are standing around like your shite doesn't stink."

"I'd rather be up at Fort William," said Sentinel Sinclair.

"Aye," Sergeant Hendrie agreed—he was a miserable Englishman from London. "Why in God's name did Colonel Hill send us here?"

After three days of listening to the grumblings in the ranks, Kier had heard enough. "A soldier's place is not to question. We're here and that's the end of it." He moved to the edge of the group of dragoons and stood alone with his tankard.

Nearby, Glenlyon was sitting on a plaid beside his niece, drinking from a flask. Kier didn't have to guess to know the captain was totting a bit of whisky. As usual, ale was too weak for the likes of the old crow. It was no secret the captain enjoyed his spirit. That's why, though he was a laird, at the age of sixty he was engaged in the service of King William of Orange rather than retired and warming his toes before home's hearth.

Across the fire, Alasdair MacIain MacDonald stood and clapped his hands. "Where's the piper and the fiddler? This gathering is as merry as a funeral procession. Let's liven it up and show our guests how Clan Iain Abrach celebrates a roasted pig."

"Here, here," bellowed Glenlyon, holding up his flask.

Kier raised his tankard aloft as well. He looked across the fire to Miss Skye expectantly. Would she entertain dancing with a Campbell lieutenant? She was sitting on a plaid with her parents. Tommy, who had been relieved of his duty at the spit, pulled his sister's hand and yanked her toward the musicians. And with the music, clansmen and women lined up for a country dance with Tommy and Skye taking a place at the end.

"Nothing like a reel to raise a soldier's spirits, is there, Lieutenant?" asked Corporal MacPhail. At least one of the dragoons in the ranks wasn't full of vinegar.

"Indeed." Kier saluted with his cup.

"Fancy that, a mob of cutthroats making merry," said Smith.

Kier eyed the lout with a leer. "Haud yer wheesht."

The sentinel batted his hand through the air and guffawed. "Christ. You're a Campbell, sir. You have cause to hate these folk all the more."

"And you, Smith, are one step shy from spending the entire night on guard duty. Let it be known I'll not hear another ill word against our hosts." Kier downed his ale and watched while Tommy tripped over his feet as he swung his sister in a circle. The lad pulled Skye around like he was leading a heifer to market. Kier grumbled under his breath. He shouldn't care, so why did he? The regiment would be gone soon enough and Miss Skye of Clan Iain Abrach would be but a distant memory. Lasses like her were plentiful enough.

Kier groaned again. Och, lasses like Miss Skye were but jewels only found after a lifetime of searching. He knew it and he suspected every male in the Coe knew it as well. Worse, she'd most likely end up marrying some ne'er-do-well cattle reiver from the Gallows Herd. In fact, Skye's future husband could very well prey on Kier's own cattle. Lord knew the

MacIains had certainly raided his family's lands at Loch Dochart often enough. 'Twas why the army was paying a kindly visit—at least that's the only reason he could fathom for their extended stay.

Kier paced until the music ended, at which time he found himself standing directly behind the lass whose future husband would become a thorn in his side and an outlaw of the Highlands.

"May I help you, Lieutenant?" asked Hugh MacIain, sauntering up with his hand gripping the pommel of his sword.

"Ah..." Kier cleared his throat and looked to Miss Skye. "I thought I'd ask the lass for a turn. After all, her father has been kind enough to provide me with a berth."

"You'd best rejoin your ranks. The bleaters mightn't ken what to do when their shepherd is kicking up his heels with a local lass."

"He's a Campbell," said a woman seated a few paces away. "Watch out for daggers hidden up his sleeves."

Kier pulled back his cuffs for all to see. "I beg your pardon, but I was under the impression this was a friendly gathering."

"Bloody oath it is!" shouted the laird, roughhewn as he was. "Hugh, stand down. The lieutenant is welcome to dance as are any other dragoons who have a notion to take a turn with one of our Highland maids. Blast it all, I said we would show hospitality and I meant every word."

Kier turned away from Hugh and bowed to Skye. The poor lass was redder than a rose in full bloom. He offered his hand. "Forgive me for making you uncomfortable. I just felt it time to ease tensions a bit."

Her eyes twinkled as she rested her fingers in his palm. "If anything, tensions have risen higher, sir."

And she was right. Not a single couple joined them. In fact, it had grown so quiet, the crackling of the fire and the creak from the spit were the only sounds.

"Come wife." The clan chief lumbered to his feet. "Let us kick up our heels with the lieutenant."

Kier bit the inside of his cheek. If nothing else, MacIain was making a herculean effort to ensure angst between government and Jacobite was kept to a minimum. Though Kier only knew Alasdair MacIain MacDonald by reputation, his effort to be accommodating surprised him. A year ago, if anyone had told him he'd be in the MacIain camp dancing a reel, he'd have laughed so hard he would have spit out his teeth.

Not to be shown up by his father, Hugh pulled his sister-in-law into line just as the music began. Kier bowed as Miss Skye curtseyed, though she kept her gaze lowered. When they turned and he offered her his palm, the swish of her skirts brushed his ankles, heightening his awareness. Tingles fired up the back of his calves as they joined elbows and skipped in a circle. She'd pulled her hair up and framed her face with ringlets. Clearly, the lass had made an effort with her appearance this eve. Did she have an eye for one of the MacIain men?

Kier's stomach tightened into a knot as he returned to the line and watched her face—watched to see if she was searching for another.

As if she could hear his thoughts, she raised her lids and met his gaze. Then she quickly glanced back to her feet as if she didn't want him to know she'd looked.

Kier's heart thumped rapidly and when they again met for a circle, he inclined his lips toward her ear. "You look radiant this eve."

Another blush flooded her cheeks. "Thank you."

"You did something special with your hair."

She smiled. Dear Lord, a radiant, blossoming smile that tickled his insides. "Ma put it up in rags this morn afore I went to the weaver's shop."

Och, aye. Kier's sisters had worn rags to bed many a night, though they'd had servants to style their tresses come morn.

The reel ended all too soon. Kier reached for Skye's hand and dipped into a bow, hovering over it. "I thank you, miss." The fingers caressing the rough pads of his palm were so soft and delicate, he hadn't a mind to release them. Inhaling the fragrance of roses, he licked his lips and closed his eyes, hankering to kiss her.

"That's enough of that," said Jimmy, pulling Miss Skye away by the elbow. "I reckon the pork's ready."

As Kier straightened, he let her fingers slip from his grasp. His palm feeling cold and empty, he stared after her dumbly as she left with her father.

Then he blinked.

He'd nearly kissed a MacIain lassie's bonny hand.

What in God's name has come over me?

***

Though sitting with her family, Skye felt utterly alone while she picked at the succulent shreds of roast pork. Why had the lieutenant asked her to dance? And now what did the clan think of her? She couldn't allow herself to look anywhere aside from her plate. Everyone was staring like she had leprosy. Worse, her heart had nearly thundered out of her chest while she was dancing with Mr. Campbell.

Campbell!

For the love of everything holy, why couldn't that man, with such an unnerving and commanding presence, be a MacIain or a Stewart from Appin or a Cameron? Why did that man, with eyes more beautiful than a glassy loch on a summer's day, have to be the son of a Campbell laird, no less?

And why the devil had he set his sights on her this eve? She was but a lowly maid, generations removed from being a chieftain's heir. Though they were presently occupying the same soil, they were separated by a divide wider than the Highlands. Mr. Campbell was not only a member of a clan that had spent centuries praying on MacDonalds and MacIains alike, he was a soldier of William of Orange. Kier Campbell was most likely a Protestant as well.

Skye made the mistake of looking up and nearly died. Holy Moses, the lieutenant was staring at her from across the bonfire. With darting glimpses from the corners of her eyes, she glanced around to see if anyone else had noticed. Thank heavens the pork had been cooked to perfection and the clansmen and women had reverted to eating and laughing as if a Campbell hadn't taken her hand after the dance and *nearly* kissed it.

Good Lord, what would she have done if he had?
Melted into a heap of nerves, for certain.

Skye shifted a bit so the next time she looked up, she'd see her scruffy brother rather than the rugged warrior wearing a red coat. A *dragoon*. A man who was an enemy to all she held dear.

"I reckon we need a song!" bellowed the great clan chief.

Under most circumstances, Skye would have beamed with such an announcement, but presently, she curved her spine and shrank lower. *Please pick someone else.*

"Miss Skye, I can still see you, lass. Do not be bashful. Come up here and give us a tune." The laird clapped his hands. "I'm certain Glenlyon will appreciate a lark's voice such as yours."

Ma gave her a nudge. "Go on, lass."

Groaning, Skye stood and moved beside the fiddler.

"*Mo Ghile Mear*," said Mistress NicGilleasbuig, asking for "My Gallant Hero". Of course, the chieftain's wife wouldn't ask for a Gaelic fighting song or the one about the lovely flowers or another ditty wishing the men well with their fishing.

Skye gulped. Most of the Gaelic songs she knew were love songs of sorts—definitely nothing she wanted to sing in the company of a regiment of dragoons.

After the fiddler played an introduction, just as Skye opened her mouth to sing, Lieutenant Campbell stepped directly into her line of sight. Her throat constricted and she couldn't make a single sound.

Blast him.

She covered her mouth and shook her head.

The fiddler lowered his instrument. "Och, let us start again, shall we?"

Skye gave him a nod and kept her gaze lowered. This time, the first verse came out fine, but she was staring at dirt, definitely not the posture Mistress NicGilleasbuig would expect from her. Clenching her fists, Skye raised her chin. Blast it all, the lieutenant stood there like he'd never heard a Gaelic ballad in his life. But she wasn't going to humiliate herself yet again. She took in a deep breath and watched the officer as she sang the last refrain:

He's my champion, my gallant hero
He's my king, a gallant hero
I've found neither rest nor fortune
Since my hero sailed far, far away
Alas, I will always love my hero, my bonny beau.

As the final note faded on the breeze, the soldiers offered the loudest applause. Skye looked to the laird who applauded, nodding his approval. Gulping back a sigh of relief, she returned to her plaid.

"That was lovely, Miss Skye." Good Lord, didn't the lieutenant realize he ought to stay on the far side of the blaze? She gave Mr. Campbell a reticent smile. "Thank you."

He, in turn, grinned broadly. It wasn't a silly grin, but a masculine grin that made the raging bonfire pale in comparison. "Would you care to take a stroll around the grounds with me?"

"I beg your pardon, young pup," said Da. "Have you been dipping into the whisky with Glenlyon?"

Mr. Campbell shook his head. "No, sir. Just thought I might stretch my legs a bit."

"My daughter can walk with you if Tommy chaperones," said Ma.

Skye shook her head. "Och, Tommy doesn't want to stroll with the likes of us."

The lad hopped to his feet. "Sure I do. And I'll be looking for a *seilie* fairy. Malcolm told me his ma saw one by the river two nights ago."

"And Malcolm breathes fire out both sides of his mouth," said Skye.

"I reckon tonight's a good night for a fairy spotting," said Mr. Campbell, taking her elbow. "Tell me, what are the signs there are fairies about?"

Skye followed, rolling her eyes to the heavens. "Don't get him started."

"Ice crystals," said Tommy.

It seemed no one was interested in listening to a word Skye had to say. And as she expected, her brother ran ahead and paid them no mind while Mr. Campbell strolled along like he hadn't a care in the world, leading her away from the security of the crowd.

"Your song was moving," he said, his voice soft and deep, making gooseflesh rise across her skin.

Skye shrugged. "I've been singing since I was a wee one, I suppose."

"Did you have lessons?"

"None."

"Well then, you are a rare and natural talent."

"My thanks." Skye stopped and looked up to his face made shadowy by the moonlight above. "We shouldn't be here, you ken."

He chuckled with a nod. "You are most likely right."

"Then why ask me to take a stroll, and in front of clan and kin?"

"Don't ken, honestly." His mouth twisted. "After you finished singing, my legs took over and there I was, asking for a harmless promenade around the grounds. Not to worry, lass. With the moonlight, we can be seen well enough."

"That almost makes it worse. I wouldn't want Mistress Fiona spreading gossip about…ah…" Skye swiped a hand across her mouth. "With luck, everyone will forget about it by the morrow."

Mr. Campbell reached for her hand. "I shan't forget. That's for certain."

Her palms grew suddenly moist, her mouth dry. Skye doubted she'd ever forget how she felt when his deep voice had made such a simple request—a mere stroll, though it was certainly not a declaration of intent to court. Nonetheless, in an instant, her skin had tingled combined with a fluttering low in her belly. No man she'd ever met had such an effect on her insides.

Why this man?

But her thoughts went completely blank and her breath caught when Mr. Campbell bowed over her hand, his warm breath caressing the back of it. Gradually, he closed the distance and pressed his lips to her flesh—warm, deliciously soft lips touched her skin with hot fervor as if he were branding a lasting impression into the back of her hand.

Her knees turned to utter mush while the same heat from her hand rushed through her body and pooled in her most sacred nether parts. In disbelief, she stared as he straightened and grinned, his white teeth glowing, making her insides swarm all the more.

Blast him.

Skye drew her hand over her heart, wanting to extend the sensation, wanting her skin to tingle like that forever. "How did you do that?"

"I beg your pardon? How did I do what, exactly?"

"How…how did you make me *feel* like that?"

He stepped nearer and again took her hand. But this time, he pressed her palm against his chest—a very hard, very broad chest. "Is your heart racing like mine?"

Indeed, his heart was thumping just as fervently as hers. "Aye," she whispered, forcing herself to pull her hand away. "But it cannot be. You and I might as well be dog and cat. Nothing good can come of this, this…whatever you want to call it."

"I think—"

"No!" Skye skittered from him, thrusting out her palm. "I'm going back now afore you make my heart thump clear out of my chest. 'Tis just not natural."

Chapter Four

"Take aim," Kier shouted, raising his sword above his head.

Kneeling, the musketeers trained their weapons on the straw targets the men had fashioned that morn.

"Fire!"

The flintlocks clicked before blasts of gunfire boomed from a dozen muskets.

"Affix bayonets," Kier shouted, looking to the targets to gauge who had hit their mark. "Charge!"

Bellowing their war cry, the men attacked the straw rounds with thrusts aimed at the heart.

"Robertson, you not only missed your target with your shot, you're too low with your thrust." Kier marched up to the sentinel and relieved him of his weapon. "What in God's name were you aiming at?"

"The target, sir."

"I beg your pardon? You're supposed to aim for the heart. In my estimation, you've just emasculated your foe. If you don't kill him now, he'll creep into your camp in the dark of night and cut off your cock."

"Beg your pardon, sir, but that coil of straw doesn't look anything like the enemy."

"Have you no imagination? Tell me, where is your heart, Robertson?"

The Englishman pointed to his chest. "Right here, sir."

Kier addressed the target. "Then where on this round of straw would your opponent's heart be, given a man the same size?"

Robertson tapped the target with his finger. "'Bout there." At least he wasn't a complete unmitigated nincompoop.

"Observe." Kier bared his teeth, lunged and buried the bayonet deep into the target's assumed heart. Regaining his composure, he pulled the weapon out and shouldered it with the muzzle pointed upward. "Are there any questions?"

"No, sir."

"Remember, bayonet thrusts are intended to kill, not to maim. Aim for the heart. For a man stabbed in the leg can still kill you or live to fight you another day. Understood?"

"Yes, sir!" bellowed the musketeers.

"Charge your weapons, men. We'll go again for the benefit of Mr. Robertson."

Throughout the practice, Kier kept an eye on Tommy who looked on from behind a sycamore. And after he dismissed the men to fall into ranks for a marching drill, he sauntered toward the tree. "Tell me lad, what have you learned after all you've seen this day?"

"You kent I was here the whole time?"

"Aye. Not much escapes me."

Tommy eyed Kier's musket with a glint of longing in his eyes. "Would you have a moment to give me a go, sir?"

"Even though I wear a red coat?"

"But you're not like the others."

"What say you? Why do you think that?"

The lad kicked a stone. "You don't say mean things...and at the gathering, you had two sentinels help with turning the spit. I think you're affable even if Da says I shouldn't trust you."

"Do you now?" Kier swallowed his urge to laugh. If the roles were reversed, he'd probably tell his kin to give the MacIains a wide berth. He'd faced them in battle too many times to ever completely let down his guard as far as Clan Iain Abrach was concerned. He removed the musket from his shoulder and took the boy to the firing line. "Let's see what you know, lad. Tell me how a man handles his musket afore he ever thinks of shooting it."

Tommy twisted his mouth. "He cleans it?"

"Aye, but afore that, he needs to ken how to take care of the weapon so he doesn't blow his foot off—or his head or the head of a friend." Dropping to his knee, Kier gave the lad a lesson in musket safety and only after doing so did he produce a powder horn and a lead ball.

After charging it, the ten-year-old raised the musket to his shoulder and set his sights, the weapon practically dwarfing him.

"Hold the barrel steady and line up with the bullseye," said Kier.

"Aye, sir. Can I shoot now?"

"Pull the trigger nice and slow."

Boom!

With Kier's next blink, Tommy stumbled backward and fell on his arse. Kier crossed his arms and stood over the boy. "Your feet weren't planted."

"I did what you said."

Kier offered his hand. "You may have thought you did what I said, but you weren't ready for the kick, otherwise you wouldn't have fallen."

Tommy took the hand and scrambled to his feet. "Och, I'll not stumble next time."

"Very, well. Charge your weapon."

With a very serious pinch to his brow, the lad went about setting up for another shot. Kier stood a good four paces behind and crossed his arms, looking on with a discerning eye.

Tommy raised the musket and pulled back the hammer.

Movement came from the left.

Kier lunged.

The trigger clicked.

"Sto-o-o-op!"

As the blast erupted, Kier batted the barrel downward.

Tommy skittered backward, tugging the weapon away. "Wha—?"

Ahead, Miss Skye stood, her arms laden with a basket of wool.

"What did I say is the first rule about handling a musket?" Kier yelled, his heart racing. The little imp nearly shot his sister.

Tommy's mouth dropped open. "But she wasn't there…I-I didn't mean…"

"Nay, you didn't mean, did you?" Kier took the gun from the lad's grasp. "And that's exactly why I drilled you on safety in the first instance."

Skye neared with her basket in tow. "I'm sorry. He looked so happy. It was my fault."

Kier gave her a look. "It is always the musketeer's duty to ensure he is firing at something that needs to be shot and that most definitely is not you, miss."

Tommy's shoulders sagged as he hung his head. "I'd never hurt my sister."

Discarding her basket, Miss Skye kneeled and grasped her brother by the shoulders. "I ken you wouldn't. But Mr. Campbell is right. You must be fully aware of your surroundings afore you shoot. Do you understand?"

The lad kicked a stone, sniffing back tears. "Aye."

"Very well. Ma needs you at the cottage." Skye mussed his hair. "Run along then."

After the lad left, she shot Kier a bitter leer and stood.

He felt like a heel. "It was important to stress the severity of his mistake." Why should he feel badly? He'd just kept the lass from being shot, especially if Tommy's aim hadn't been spot on to the target.

Her fingers brushed the basket handle. "Was it?"

Kier pulled it from her grasp. "It was. I would have reacted the same if Tommy had been my own kin."

With a haughty turn of her head, she started toward the chieftain's manor. "So, you're not discerning as to whose children at whom you're shouting?"

"Of course I am...I mean, I'm not. Had the lad misfired, you could be flat on your back with a lead ball in your skull."

"Charming."

"Muskets are not toys."

"I'll say. If man hadn't invented the musket, Dugal MacIain might still be alive."

A flash of hot ire spread across the back of Kier's neck. "Who is Dugal MacIain?"

"Not anyone I'd expect you to know."

Kier grumbled under his breath and followed the woman into the weaver's shop. Who the devil was this man? Someone who'd spoken for Skye's hand? Good God, now his innards were twisting into knots. He set the basket down on the table with more force than necessary.

"I beg your pardon, but I'll need to use that again. There's no point in taking out your ire on a wee basket."

Kier drew in a deep breath, his gaze sweeping across the shop. Thank heavens they were alone and no one else had heard the lass's chiding. "The bloody basket may not have deserved to be manhandled, but Tommy needed a firm warning."

Skye pursed her lips and nodded. "I suppose I should thank you."

"Not necessary."

"If there is nothing else, I've work to do."

"Forgive me for intruding." He moved toward her, his fingers brushing her woolen skirts. "But before I leave, tell me, who was Dugal MacIain?"

"Were you present during the Battle of Dunkeld?"

"Aye, I carried the standard for my father. I was but one and twenty at the time."

"I was sixteen."

"And Dugal?"

"Nineteen." She sighed, drawing a hand to her forehead.

"And you cared for him?"

She nodded. "But Da didn't ken."

"What happened?"

"I'm sure you're aware of the MacIain raid on Glenlyon's lands."

"Aye." Kier rolled his hand encouraging her to continue.

"After the battle was lost, the laird sought vengeance."

"And he stole Glenlyon's prized stallion."

"The stallion is sterile."

"I'd heard."

Miss Skye crossed her arms and tilted up her chin. "Alasdair set Glenlyon's stable afire on account of his merciless murder of Dugal."

Kier knit his brows. "But the lad rode into battle, did he not?"

"He did, and he was captured. But as the Campbells were mustering the prisoners into the wagon, Glenlyon stopped Dugal…and…"

A clammy chill coursed across Kier's skin while the memory hit him between the eyes like a brick. Dear God. He'd been there. He's seen the barbarous act. "Glenlyon…"

"Slit his throat."

"And hence the raid."

"Aye," Skye's whispered reply was barely audible. A tear slipped from her eye.

"Jesu." Kier pulled the lass into his arms and cradled her head against his heart. "In this moment, all the centuries of feuding between our clans amounts to nothing more than madness." It made no sense to tell her he'd lost kin in that raid as well. Christ. It all seemed so senseless.

She took in a stuttered breath as she trembled in his arms. "I fear it will never end."

"I ken, lass." Aye, Kier knew she was right. Rumors were rife among the ranks of King William and the Master of Stair's maniacal desire to bring the Highlands into compliance. Jacobitism would no longer be tolerated. True, Colonel Hill had talked about leading a peaceful transition, but tensions at Fort William were higher than Kier had ever seen them. Alasdair MacIain MacDonald might have signed the oath of fealty to the king, but other than ink on a bit of parchment, nothing had changed.

"And what are you doing here?" Miss Skye asked. "Why is Glenlyon sleeping less than a mile from the laird's door?"

"We're awaiting orders. That is all."

"But what if something bad happens? What if the soldiers have too much to drink and a feud breaks out?"

"I won't let that happen."

"What if it does?"

"Then I will protect you." Kier pressed his lips against her crown and closed his eyes. "I swear on my life, I'll not let harm befall you or your family. You've taken me in. You've shown me kindness and for that I am in your debt."

"If only Glenlyon's orders would come then we would be rid of him. But..." Her hands slipped around his waist and pulled him tight, looking him in the eye. "But I want you to stay."

Gasping, his heart thumped like the beat of a snare drum. With those words, something burst in Kier's chest, something wonderful, sending the brilliance of sunshine beaming through his entire body. His fingers slipped up and threaded through her silken tresses while his lips caressed her temple, her cheek. He hovered there for a moment, inhaling her scent, willing her to raise her chin. When she did, his entire body turned molten. He needed no more encouragement. As he slid his fingers along her jaw, he met those delicate lips with a kiss. Connecting with a burst of energy, it was as if their very souls merged. Never in his life had he been knocked into fervent passion by the mere joining of lips. And with the lass's wee moan came an involuntary tightening low in his gut.

Backing her toward the wall, he deepened the kiss, craving friction, wild with the need to feel the softness of her breasts mold into his chest, the need to do far more than that—to touch her, to thrust his hips forward and brush his loins against the folds of her skirts.

A door opening registered faintly, though Kier paid it no mind.

"Lieutenant Campbell, I must bid you release Miss Skye this very instant!"

The lass jumped from his arms, her hand covering her mouth. "Mistress NicGilleasbuig."

Chapter Five

"Sir, I must *insist* you return to your regiment with haste!" Alasdair MacIain's wife thrust her finger toward the door.

Kier turned redder than the ball of scarlet yarn in Skye's basket. "I beg your pardon, miss." Shooting her a flustered gaze, he dipped into a curt bow then hastened out the door.

Skye gulped and shifted her attention to her mistress. "Forgive me. I have no idea what came over me."

The woman's features pinched with outrage. "I should say not. Do you realize that man is a *Campbell?*" Mistress NicGilleasbuig spat out Kier's name as if it were a vile curse.

Skye pressed her palms together and tapped her lips. "'Twasn't what you think. I—"

"What *I* think? Tell me what isn't scandalous about a wee maid swooning in the arms of a dragoon with her lips fused with his?"

"But—"

"Make no bones about it, we may be extending hospitality to Glenlyon and his mob of upstarts, but when they march out of the Coe, that will be the end of it." Mistress NicGilleasbuig threw up her hands. "I must speak to your mother at once."

"No. Please, no. Do not make more of this than it is."

"Exactly what did I miss? You were swooning in the man's arms!"

"It was merely the moment. I-I had a lapse in judgement."

The older woman shifted her fists to her hips. "I ken you're young and impressionable, and that braw warrior turns heads everywhere he sets foot, but you must always remember your roots. You must put clan and kin afore a bonny face such as his."

"Aye, Mistress." Skye wrung her hands. "But, please. Can this remain between us?"

Mistress NicGilleasbuig sniffed and narrowed her eyes. "Only if you promise not to let that man's braw looks mar your judgement in the future. I ken you to be a sensible lass, but if I catch wind of one more inappropriate act, I shall have no choice but to have words with your mother."

Drawing her hands over her heart, Skye dipped into a curtsey and bowed her head. "Thank you. Thank you ever so much, Matron."

"But—I *will* mention it to Hugh. He's near enough to the lieutenant in age. I'll have him issue a warning."

Skye gulped, her shoulders tensing. *Hugh?* "Do you think it necessary? I—"

"Of course it is necessary! I wouldn't have said so if I didn't believe it to be true. That dragoon needs to be forewarned." The lady gestured toward the loom. "Now set to work. You've idled away enough of this day already."

***

Standing shoulder to shoulder with his men, Kier tossed the dice into a cup and rattled them around. "Come ye bloody sixes."

Though there was no formal alehouse in Glencoe, like all Scottish settlements, there was a brewhouse where ale was made and stored in casks. With the arrival of the regiment, it didn't take long for the brewhouse to become a place for the soldiers to congregate after long days of marching.

He rolled the dice onto the top of the barrel the men used as a makeshift table and groaned. "A pair of miserable twos."

"Luck's not with you this day, is it?" asked Hugh MacIain, sauntering through the crowd. He bellied up to the barrel, scowling at the two dragoons Kier had been playing with. "Give us a moment, would you?"

Kier knew exactly why MacIain had sought him out. It hadn't taken the blighter long. "Had a word with your mother did you?"

"I did."

Taking a drink of ale, Kier pondered his response. "I have no quarrel with you."

"No?"

"No."

MacIain inched a bit closer. "You should have thought about that afore you kissed Miss Skye."

Aye, and Kier had been kicking himself ever since. "I won't disagree with you there."

"And what are your intentions?"

"Bloody hell." He threw up his hands. "It was but a kiss."

"Was it now?" Hugh rapped his knuckles atop the barrel. "Without her father's consent? You ken as well as I a wee kiss leads to more."

Kier pursed his lips. "It will not here."

"It had better not."

"Understood."

Hugh picked up the cup and plunked in the dice, then shook it. "You ken if you hurt the lass, you'll pay tenfold." He rolled a pair of sixes.

Kier raised his cup. "It appears your luck is a mite better than mine, my friend."

Grabbing his forearm, Hugh leaned in. "We're no friends and I want your word you'll stay away from the lass."

Kier narrowed the gap, his nose but a hair's breadth from MacIain's. "That's a bit difficult given I'm staying with her kin."

Hugh squeezed his fingers.

The lieutenant met the man's dark-eyed stare for a moment. It wasn't so long ago they were on opposite sides of a battle, the guards of their swords locked in a duel of strength. If he weren't in the Coe on army business, he might just invite the scrapper outside for a spar. "Och, you ken the lass is safe with me."

"That's what I wanted to hear." Hugh released his grip.

Kier's shoulders tensed. On second thought, perhaps he ought to give the heir a bit of a rib. He grasped MacIain's upper arm and gave it a squeeze. "I see you haven't gone soft since we last locked swords."

Hugh yanked his arm away. "Swinging an ax will do that to a man."

"We could use a fella like you in our ranks." Leaning in, Kier waggled his eyebrows.

"And that will happen when hell freezes."

Kier laughed. "I always did like you, MacIain. You were never one to mince words. Mayhap we can go a couple rounds for the captain—I'd wager he'd recruit you on the spot."

"And you're full of shite." Hugh thwacked him on the back. "Just remember your promise."

Chapter Six

At the table, Skye sliced the bread for the evening meal. She'd been paid with two loaves and the one beneath her fingertips was still warm. Her mouth watered as the tasty aroma wafted around her.

After a polite knock on the door, Mr. Campbell entered. "Good evening, MacDonalds."

When he grinned at her, she quickly shifted her attention to the bread, ferociously sawing with the knife.

"Marched yourself up a hunger, did you?" asked Da with a curl of pipe smoke billowing through his nose.

If Da's curt question irritated the lieutenant, Mr. Campbell didn't show it. He turned and hung his bonnet on the peg, resting his musket and sword beneath it. "I'm surprised not to see Tommy inside."

"He's not in the paddock?" asked Ma.

"I sent him up the Lochan trail. Now the snow has melted, I though the sheep could use a good graze." Da pulled out his pocket watch—the only piece of jewelry he owned. He sucked in a hiss. "Come to think on it, the lad should have returned hours ago."

"He's most likely daydreaming again," said Ma. "I'll wager the sheep are scattered."

"The north wind's blowing a gale," said Mr. Campbell.

Skye stilled her knife. "And Tommy's up in the hills?"

The lieutenant pulled his bonnet from the peg. "I'll fetch him."

"'Tis nearly dusk. Do you ken the trail?" asked Ma.

"I do." Skye brushed her fingers on her apron and stood. "I'm going with you."

"Take the lantern," said Da, with increasing urgency in his voice. "If you're not back within the hour, I'll alert the clan."

Mr. Campbell secured his musket strap over his shoulder. "We'll find him, sir."

Ma grabbed the lantern from the mantel and handed it to Skye. "Haste, now, while there's some daylight remaining."

Once outside, the lieutenant made quick work of saddling his horse. "We've no choice but to ride double. We'll move faster that way."

Skye gulped and looked back toward the chieftain's manse. If the mistress caught wind that she was riding double with Mr. Campbell, there'd be hell to pay. And Mistress NicGilleasbuig had been right. Skye had been reckless and had paid no mind to her actions in the weaver's shop. Worse, now she had no choice but to take the man up on his offer. No question, the horse would be faster and they needed to find Tommy, daydreaming or not.

She wrapped her arisaid over her head and shoulders and pushed away her misgivings. Mr. Campbell gave her a boost, then she sat across the gelding's withers while the lieutenant mounted behind her. Skye's stilly heart started to flutter when he reached around for the reins. Heaven's stars, he was so close, the scent of leather and spice made her head swoon. And when her shoulder pressed into the hard wall of his chest, the memory of their fleeting kiss made searing heat flood through her body with a force as powerful as the Falls of Glencoe. If only she could wrap her arms around his waist and rest her head against him. If only they weren't from feuding clans.

If only I wasn't so touched in the head. Showing no outward signs of the conflict brewing within her, Skye twisted and kept her gaze forward, grasping a handful of mane to keep herself steady. "Cross the river in the shallows, then you'll see the trail yonder." She searched the hill for any sign of Tommy, but he was not to be seen.

"Does the lad venture up here often?" Mr. Campbell asked. Had his voice always been so deep?

Skye nodded. "Aye, especially in summer. The older sheep know what's coming when we open the back gate."

"How far up does Tommy usually go?"

"A mile or two up to the lea."

"Good, then we'll be upon him in moments." Slapping his reins, the lieutenant cued the horse to a fast trot.

Skye leaned forward and clamped her fist tighter. "Tommy!" she yelled.

"Tommy!" Mr. Campbell bellowed behind her.

When there was no response, they continued up the slope, while they both continued to holler. As they summited the hill, Skye grasped Mr. Campbell's wrist. "Halt."

He pulled on the reins. "Do you see him?"

"Nay, but this is where we let the sheep graze." She twisted to look full circle, then cupped her hands around her mouth. "Tooooomeeee!"

A high-pitched whistle echoed on the wind.

Skye snapped her head toward the sound.

The lieutenant pointed upward. "It came from the outcropping."

She squinted against the setting sun. Sure enough, a flock of sheep were mustered in the distance. "Haste!"

"Hold on, lass," Mr. Campbell growled in her ear while he cued the horse for a canter. Her bum flopped askew, nearly making her fall. Gasping, Skye gave up on the clump of mane and threw her arms around the man's waist, holding on for dear life.

"Tommy?" the lieutenant yelled, slowing the horse to a walk as they neared the flock. "Where are you, lad?"

"Up here!" the lad's voice came from above.

"Good heavens." Skye peered up the steep slope all the way to the top and still didn't see her brother. "Why on earth did he climb up there?"

"I reckon we'll find out." Mr. Campbell helped her slide down, then dismounted. "Are you all right?" he shouted again.

"My leg," Tommy responded, his voice higher pitched than usual.

Skye started for the slope. "Hold on. We're coming!"

A big hand clamped on her shoulder, fingers gripping like a vise. "Stay with the horse. I don't need two injured children to haul back to your parents."

Her back shot to rigid as she faced him and thrust her fists into her hips. "I beg your pardon, but I am not a child."

Mr. Campbell's lips thinned as he met her gaze, his eyes growing dark as if he had something to say, but held it inside. He handed her the reins. "I'll be back."

"But he's my brother."

The man ignored her and set off like a boar-brained ruffian. Didn't he know she was worried half out of her mind? Tommy was stranded atop an outcropping with an injured leg? For all she knew it might be broken. He could be stuck. The lad needed his sister. And moreover, they'd kissed one day prior. Had that meant nothing to the man? Men didn't shower a woman with affection and then refer to her as a child. Skye chewed her lip. The blasted kiss had done nothing but haunt her and since, they'd barely even locked gazes—not that she could have done anything if he had tried to speak to her, or touch her, or place another kiss on her mouth…with those pillow-soft, masculine lips.

Heaven's stars, I'm daft.

Quickly returning her attention to the urgency of the situation, Skye watched the lieutenant climb the slope while pebbles and dirt showered behind him. Alas, encumbered by petticoats and skirts, she never would have been able to move so quickly.

Though concerned about the lad, Kier was glad to have the diversion of scaling the outcropping. He'd referred to Skye as a child for his own edification. God save him, having the lass ride between his arms and his thighs was more than a mere officer could be expected to bear without feeling something. The problem was he felt a hell of a lot more than a twinge of desire. A full-on blast from an iron furnace was more apt.

No matter how much Kier wanted to spite Hugh MacIain and plunder the woman who'd ridden in his arms, he couldn't do it. Poor Miss Skye was beside herself with worry and the only thing Kier had managed to think about was the curve of her thigh rubbing against his cock or the tingling sensation of her delicate arm pressed against his aching chest. Christ, he needed a good run up a hundred steep slopes to curb the maniacal lust that had begun to torment his soul.

By the time he reached the top, he was breathing good and deep. "Tommy," he called out, his gaze darting across the crags.

"Here." The lad's voice sounded strained.

Glimpsing Tommy's mop of brown curls, Kier hastened over the sharp boulders. "Bloody Christmas, what in God's name are you doing up here?"

The lad bared his teeth with a grimace of pain. "Chasing after *seilie* fairies. I kent I saw one."

Kier studied the lad's leg, wedged beneath a big rock. If only he could slap the child on the back of the head and berate him. He'd abandoned the flock to chase after a damned dream. "What happened?"

The lad pointed to the enormous stone atop his foot. "I was climbing up this rock and it rolled back on my ankle."

Kier placed his palms on the enormous stone. The last thing he needed was to try to move it and make Tommy's injury worse. And there weren't many options as to where he could roll it since the lad was blocking the path of least resistance. "Tell you what, I'm going to need your help."

"Wha-what can I do?"

"When I push up the rock, I want you to scoot back as fast as you can and pull your foot out from under there."

"Will it hurt?"

"Most likely."

Tears welled in Tommy's eyes and his lips quivered.

Kier grasped the lad's hand and squeezed it, holding the small palm to his chest. "Listen to me. I will free your leg, but I cannot do it unless you are strong for me."

"But—"

"Anything worth doing bears pain, lad. But I tell you true, you'll be a great deal worse off if I leave you here to the buzzards."

"Buzzards?" he squeaked.

"Aye, they'll swoop down and peck out your eyes if you cannot find the strength to slide back and pull your leg away." Kier gave the lad a somber stare. "Promise me. 'Tis time to bear down and be a man."

A tear dribbled down the boy's cheek. "Yes, sir."

"At the count of three?"

Tommy nodded.

Kier shifted back to the boulder. "One, two, three!" Gritting his teeth, he pushed the hunk of granite with all his might, rolling it up the adjoining rock face. Every muscle in his body strained and shook as he steadied it above the boy's leg. "Now!"

Crying out, Tommy scooted away and drew his knees under his chin.

Kier lowered the rock as gradually as possible to keep it from rolling further. If it started on a path down the hill, it would crush the lad for certain. Gingerly, he pulled his hands away. When the boulder stayed put, Kier dropped to his knees and examined Tommy's ankle.

"Is it bad?"

"'Tis swollen. Can you move your foot?"

Grimacing, Tommy gave it a try. "I reckon I moved my big toe."

"That's a good sign." Kier gave him an encouraging pat. "Can you put a wee bit of weight on it?"

Anguish stretched the lad's features as he leaned forward and placed his foot square on the ground. "Mother's bricks, that hurts."

Kier held up a palm. "That's enough. I'll carry you down to my horse." After gathering Tommy into his arms, he gave the boy a look. "Mother's bricks?"

"Och, Da will not allow me to swear."

"Good on him." Kier winked. "Mother's bricks it is, then."

By the time Kier made it to the bottom of the hill, it was dark and Skye had lit the lantern.

The poor lass was beside herself with worry. "Tommy, are you hurt badly?"

"I can't put weight on my foot."

"His ankle is awfully swollen." Kier explained what happened while he hoisted the boy to the saddle. "The flock will scatter if we try to drive them to the croft now. 'Tis best to leave them here overnight. I'll help your father drive them back come morn."

Miss Skye agreed. The trip down the trail took a fair bit longer to traverse. Kier carried the lantern and led the horse with the lass and her brother on the back. Moreover, the wind howled and blew against them. With his hands full, Kier had naught to do but dip his chin against the gale and trudge westward. By the time they reached the cottage, the damned wind had started to blow snow sideways into their faces.

When Miss Skye opened the door, they found her father dressed in trews, wrapped in a blanket with a lantern in his hand.

The old man's jaw dropped. "You found him?"

"Up the outcropping by the Lochan clearing."

"You mean to say a sheep strayed all the way up there?"

Kier carried the lad past Jimmy to his pallet near the hearth. He wasn't about to tell the man that his son had been chasing damned fairies. "Mistress Sineag, Tommy's ankle is swollen something awful. He might need a splint."

"My poor darling." The matron collected the medicine bundle from the shelf. "Bring the lanterns. I'll need ample light."

"A big rock rolled onto my foot and pinned my ankle. Mr. Campbell found me and carried me all the way down the crag, and he led the horse, and did you ken 'tis blizzarding outside?"

Mistress Sineag kneeled beside the boy and untied his boot.

Tommy's eyes grew enormous. "Don't touch it."

Kier cleared his throat. "Remember what I said."

The lad pursed his lips and looked to his da while his mother made quick work of removing his boot and stocking. "Oh, my heavens."

Even Kier cringed. The lad's ankle was purple and the size of a shinty ball.

Tommy pulled his fists against his chest and shuddered. But when he looked a Kier, he sat taller and sucked in a breath. "I can move my big toe."

***

The hour was late when everyone finally headed for bed. Though Skye couldn't sleep. She lay on her back atop the box bed listening to her father snore. It seemed an eternity while she lay there as she grew hungrier by the moment. Aye, Ma had served up a bite of pottage, but Skye had been too worked up to eat much. Now she regretted it.

Giving up on sleep, she climbed down and wrapped a blanket around her shoulders.

Kier's bedclothes rustled while Skye sliced off a portion of bread.

"Hello," he said from his pallet in a deep whisper, his face glowing amber with the flicker of the hearth's fire.

She nibbled a bite. "Did I wake you?" she whispered back.

He sat up, the bedclothes dropping to his waist. He wore only a linen shirt, its laces open and the neckline slinging off his shoulder, the front dipping to the center of his chest.

Skye's lips parted as she drew in a shallow breath. Dark curls peeked above the V. That naughty stirring roiled through her insides again. Why on earth would a glimpse at the man's chest cause such an overreaction? Her father had a bit of hair on his chest and, in truth, Skye found Da's sparse curls a bit off putting. She shivered. Even with the fire, the cottage was chilly. "Jack Frost has brought a bitter chill."

"Indeed. It grew colder by the moment as we headed down from the Lochan trail." He pointed. "Would you mind cutting a slice of bread for me as well?"

Skye did as he asked, buttered it and took it to him.

"My thanks." He patted his pallet. "If you sit here, we can keep our voices down and avoid waking the others."

She didn't think of the consequences when she folded her legs and sat beside him just as if he was Tommy or Da, but when she stared up into those midnight blue eyes, Skye knew she was caught in the snare of the man's allure. Being close to Kier Campbell made her come alive like never before. It was as if everything in the Highlands came to a stop and they were the only two people existing in all of Christendom.

He slipped something shiny under his pillow.

"What's that?" she asked.

He gave her a dubious look and pulled out a miniature in a silver pocket frame. "'Tis a portrait of my mother. It is all I have left of her."

Skye ran her finger around the rim. "She was bonny."

"Aye, and I doubt my father will ever find another." He slid the miniature back into its hiding place, then chewed his bread while he watched her. The intensity of his stare didn't make her nervous, but rather, made her feel beautiful.

He brushed the tresses away from her face. "Bonny Miss Skye."

Heat spread across her cheeks while she took a bite of bread. "Have you ever been to the Isle of Skye? 'Tis where my grandfather was born."

"Once, 'tis a magical place. They say it is rife with fairies."

"Then Tommy would be in heaven there."

Mr. Campbell chuckled.

"Tell me more about it."

"'Tis a rich green like the Coe, rugged and stark, surrounded by the sea. Though Campbells are not welcome on MacDonald lands. My visit was to Dunvegan and the MacLeods."

"Och, MacLeods? Yet another clan that feuds with ours."

He nodded. "Mindlessness."

"Do you honestly believe so?"

"I do."

"Then why do you wear a red coat?"

"I've said it afore, my father thought a turn in the army would do me good. Prepare me to become a laird in my own right. Besides…" His gaze trailed away as if he had more to say, but was holding it inside.

"What else?"

A long sigh blew through the lieutenant's lips. "My uncle needed me to keep an eye on Glenlyon."

"I thought Glenlyon was your uncle."

"He is."

"But you have more than one uncle, of course?"

"Too many when you count all the second cousins removed and the like. The mind boggles."

"Who told you to keep an eye on the captain?"

"The Earl of Argyll."

"Oh." A shiver coursed across Skye's skin while her throat thickened. There she sat beside a man who was, in fact, the spawn of her clan's greatest enemies—someone she should despise to her core. "'Tis so odd, our being a-acquainted."

"I ken."

"You do?"

He folded the rest of his bread and stuffed it into his mouth. "Had the regiment not marched into Glencoe, I doubt we ever would have met."

Skye nodded and cupped her hand over her mouth to be doubly sure her whispers wouldn't be heard. "Mistress NicGilleasbuig made me swear I'd never kiss you again."

"Did she now?"

"Mm hmm."

"I heard the same from her son."

"From Hugh?"

Kier nodded. Moving a bit closer, he ran his finger along Skye's bottom lip, his touch so light, she felt naught but tingling. "How do you…ah…feel about that?"

"I-I don't like anyone telling me who can and who cannot be my friend."

"I'm of the same mind," he whispered, dipping his chin. "I rather like kissing you."

Skye could scarcely breathe as those full, virile lips moved closer. If only she could taste him again, press her lips to his and swoon in his arms. But they'd already created such a scandal. She placed her palm on his chest to stop him, but that only served to make her awareness soar to new heights. His flesh was afire beneath her touch. His heart beat a fierce rhythm that demanded she look up to his eyes. Her tongue went dry. Dark eyes filled with smoldering emotion stared into hers.

"Let me kiss you, Skye of Clan Iain Abrach."

She drew in an unsteady breath. "But what of the morrow? What happens when you mount your horse and ride back to your da's lands? What of our kisses then?"

His lips parted while his tongue moistened his bottom lip. Heaven help her, it was all she could do not to slide her fingers to his neck and close the distance. "Ah," he said, pulling away, the movement making Skye's hand slide down the wall of his abdomen. "It would be irresponsible of me to shower you with promises I cannot keep."

She gulped and pulled her fingers away, crossing her arms tightly as if the gesture would protect her from her own hot-blooded emotions. "Ours is a forbidden fondness."

Grazing his teeth over his bottom lip, Mr. Campbell's expression grew softer. "Forbidden and impossible and I would never want to do anything to hurt you."

"You already have." Skye lowered her hands to push to her feet, but he stopped her.

"Stay."

"But—"

"We mightn't have a future together. But honestly, who kens what the future will bring. I'm an officer in King William's army. I could be called to Flanders on the morrow and shot dead the day I set foot in France."

Her resolved waned. Why did everything have to be so confusing? Skye rocked back and raked her fingers through her hair. "You mustn't talk like that."

"No? Not when 'tis true?" He fingered a lock of her hair and held it to his nose. "I have faced Hugh MacIain in battle, sword against sword. Who was right and who was wrong? He stole Glenlyon's stallion and afore that, the captain stole a dozen head of cattle from the MacIain's grazing lands up the Devil's Staircase."

She shook her head. "It all sounds so senseless when you put it like that."

"Highland feuding is senseless. And do you think King William is going to allow it to continue when he needs conscripts to man his war in France?"

"No, and that's why the clan chiefs are signing the oath of fealty."

"Aye, after they received an order to do so from the exiled King James."

"But why should treaties and wars concern us? No king of England, Scotland and Ireland ever lifted a finger to help MacIains put food on the table or to clothe our children. All they want is our young men to fight their battles and die far away from their kin. They leave widows and orphans who pine at home whilst they beg for alms." Skye buried her face in her hands. "I hate war and feuds."

"'Tis the way of it," the lieutenant said so softly, she barely heard him. He rubbed his hand across her shoulders. "If it is any consolation, I'm of like mind. Perhaps there'll come a time when MacIain faces Campbell and shakes hands in true friendship."

Skye grasped the braw soldier's hand, then turned and faced him, pressing his fingers over her heart so he might feel the fervent beating that thundered in her breast. "I am taking your hand in this moment, Mr. Campbell. In this moment, we are but a man and a woman. There is no clan standing between us, no arms preventing you from feeling the rhythm of my heart. Am I not flesh and blood just as you are?"

His gaze met hers with a force that shot like an arrow through her blood. "You and I are kindred spirits no matter the men who sired us. Please, please call me Kier."

Before she could respond, he closed his mouth over hers while a bone-melting fire spilled through her soul. Merely the pressure of his mouth against hers gripped her heart and made it soar. This wasn't a stolen kiss in the wee hours of the night. This was a declaration of life and liberty between two tortured lovers who could never be. Even though they could never share a life together, she threw herself into the passion coursing between them and met his lips with the hunger of the starved.

She sighed as he trailed kisses down her neck, wanting more, wanting to feel everything this man had to give. Her one regret? If only they were truly alone, she could cry out with joy.

Chapter Seven

Kier cradled Skye while she nestled into his chest. His eyelids grew heavy and he reclined against the wall as he watched her sleep. Her face was so smooth and pure, he imagined angels looked like her. His chest swelled with the myriad of emotions thrumming with his every breath. Though he was a lieutenant and second in charge, Glenlyon still hadn't informed them of their purpose. Aye, they were awaiting Colonel Hill's orders, but surely the captain had an idea of their next move.

With dozens of clans yet to sign the oath of fealty to King William, it was reasonable that troops would be stationed along the western shore of the Highlands where the unruliest clans lived. Clans like the Camerons, the MacDonells, the MacDonalds and the most notorious of all, the MacIains. Indeed, Kier had firsthand experience with the latter. Clan Iain Abrach was the most flagrant, riotous mob of thieves in all of Scotland.

And there he sat with one of their daughters in his arms and he was completely smitten. It had been all he could do just to kiss the lass and restrain his hot Campbell urges. Och aye, Campbells were not entirely the righteous, honorable noblemen they purported themselves to be. They, too, lived by a code of an eye for an eye, a tooth for a tooth. When the MacIains raided, Campbells repaid in kind…though they twisted the law to their side and undertook every underhanded action to ensure they gained power with the incumbent monarch. They were as much whores to the realm as MacIains were pirates.

A loud snore rumbling from the box bed snapped Kier from his thoughts. He smoothed his palm over Skye's silken tresses and kissed her temple. If only he weren't in the army, he might take the lass and sail away to the Americas and find a home where birthright didn't matter.

But soon the cottage would stir and if Skye's parents found the lass asleep in Kier's arms there'd be hell to pay.

"Skye," he whispered.

She didn't move. Just continued to slumber like an angel.

Kier looked to the bed. If he carried her across the floor and hoisted her to the top, he'd run a great risk of waking Jimmy and Sineag. On the opposite wall, Tommy appeared to be cozy enough on his pallet, and it would be like Skye to slip down and tend her brother in the night. Making his decision, Kier gathered the lass in his arms and carried her over to the boy. Gently he rested her on her side and kissed her again. Then he took his tartan blanket and draped it over her.

After he slipped back to his own pallet, Kier rested, content he'd done the right thing.

But his contentment was short lived.

It seemed like he'd been asleep for two minutes when a great deal of shouting tore him from a pleasant dream. In the blink of an eye, Kier hopped to his feet, facing the ire of Mistress Sineag and the woman's bright red face. She shoved his blanket into his chest. "Exactly what, pray tell was *this* doing atop my daughter?"

Skye looked stricken. "Ma—"

"And, you, young lady. What in heaven's name prompted you to sneak down from your bed when there is a *Campbell dragoon* sleeping in the cottage?"

"This is scandalous!" Jimmy bellowed, springing from the box bed and wrapping a kilt around his hips. "I kent bringing a Campbell backstabber into my home would come to no good. Good God, strolls around the grounds and now this?"

Kier threw up his palms. "I have no idea what you think happened here last eve, but I assure you, your daughter's virtue is still intact."

Skye dashed across the floor and flung her arms around him. "Kier is right. He has acted honorably."

Mistress Sineag's face grew redder. "You call him familiar and embrace him?" She drew the back of her hand to her forehead. "Lord save me, I shall have one of my spells."

Jimmy grabbed Skye by the arm and yanked her away from Kier with such force, she stumbled to her knees. "Never touch that man again." He shifted a hateful gaze to the lieutenant. "Get out, ye scoundrel. If you weren't a guest of the laird, I'd skin you alive I would!"

Kier bowed and hastened to collect his things. Before leaving, he faced them. "Forgive my impertinence, sir. My only concern was Miss Skye's comfort."

"Never come back!" the matron yelled as Kier pushed out the door.

"Mr. Campbell!" Skye called after him, her voice shrill.

Marching away, Kier stopped for a moment and listened.

"He did nothing but put a blanket over my shoulders and you accused him of taking advantage?" Skye's voice was filled with vinegar. "You are contemptable. How dare you fault me? I am a grown woman and fully capable of taking care of myself."

"Oh, you think so, do you now?" said Jimmy.

Kier had heard enough. The lass would be fine. In a couple of days her parents would forgive her and all would be forgotten. Good Lord, how would they have reacted if they'd found him kissing the lass? He strode toward the marching paddock. This was for the best. He knew as he cradled her in his arms last eve that his actions had been wrong. The whole bloody affair was wrong. Hell, it wasn't even an affair. It was more like an inexplicable attraction. Christ, men had been attracted to women they shouldn't throughout history. *Look at Helen of Troy and the bumbling mess that made.*

***

Skye spent the next few days stewing. One moment she'd be so enraged she could spit and the next, the burden of guilt would creep up her spine and make her refrain from speaking her mind. She had no idea how she'd ended up on the pallet next to Tommy that night. Only Kier could have moved her there and the proof was the blanket covering her shoulders. Her parents hated Campbells so much they couldn't stand the thought of their daughter having any sort of friendship with one.

Worse, it seemed every time Skye looked out the window of the weaver's shop she saw Kier marching his men. When she ran errands, she inevitably bumped into him. Having him in Glencoe was tearing her apart on the inside. She couldn't even say hello without turning heads. And yet, after twelve days, Captain Campbell of Glenlyon still hadn't received his miserable orders. He'd most likely never receive orders. The regiment would be billeted to Glencoe forever. They'd end up building a fort in the laird's courtyard and Skye would grow old pining for Kier, throwing him forlorn looks and listening to endless chiding by Mistress NicGilleasbuig and Ma.

Sweeping the floor where Kier's pallet had been, the broom brushed something shiny. Skye looked up to see if anyone had noticed. Da sat smoking his pipe and whittling a stick while Ma sat darning socks. Because Tommy's ankle was still healing, the lad was still using the pallet by the hearth. He was playing with a set of soldiers Da had whittled ages ago. Skye bent down and brushed the dirt off the object, recognizing it at once. It was the miniature of Kier's mother. Turning toward the wall, Skye picked it up and slipped it into her pocket just as a knock came at the door.

After a long pause, Ma looked to Da. "Are you planning to answer yet this eve?"

"A man cannot enjoy a moment's peace." Grumbling, the old man set his tools aside and lumbered to the door.

"Good evening, Jimmy," said a deep voice—though not Kier's voice.

"Hugh." Da sounded delighted. "To what do we owe this kindly visit?"

"My father has requested Miss Skye come sing for his dinner guests at the manse, if it wouldn't be too much trouble."

"Sing for Alasdair?" Ma scurried to the door. "It would be no trouble at all. Come, Skye. You mustn't keep the laird waiting."

She glanced down at her dirty apron. "But I look a fright."

Huffing, Ma strode over and pinched Skye's cheeks. "You look lovely, dear. You always do." She pulled the apron tie. "Let's just slip this off and pat down those flyaways."

As Hugh escorted her to the manse, Skye's mind raced. He didn't say much and seemed to be preoccupied, which suited her just fine. "Who are the laird's guests?" she finally asked.

"Same as they have been for nearly a fortnight now. Glenlyon and his officers."

Her stomach jumped. That meant Kier would be there. With luck, she might be able to return his miniature. Perhaps she'd happen upon the chance to apologize for her parents' abhorrent behavior as well.

Hugh opened the door and gestured toward the dining hall. Skye had never been a guest there, but had been a servant before she started working in the weaver's shop. The laird's laughter resounded through the corridor.

"Sounds like he's making merry," Skye said.

"Or giving a good pretense of it." Hugh straightened and walked ahead. "We're in luck, gentlemen. Miss Skye has agreed to sing for us."

Alasdair MacIain clapped his hands. "Good on you, lass."

She stepped around Hugh, looking at the long table set with fine dinnerware and delicate goblets filled with wine.

"Aye," said Captain Glenlyon giving her the once-over with his shifty eyes. "I so enjoyed your performance at the gathering, I'd hoped to listen again afore my orders arrive."

Skye nodded, panning her gaze across the faces until she met Kier's intense midnight blues. The corners of her mouth turned up as he gave her a friendly nod.

This time, she filled with confidence as she sang a Celtic love song. Though she tried to remain impartial and shift her gaze to each guest, by the end of the ballad, the only man in the room became Kier Campbell and the intensity of his devilish stare. At least until the applause. In a blink, Skye snapped her gaze away and bowed her head.

"Och, aye the lass has a set of pipes," said Glenlyon, practically clapping louder than the laird.

Kier applauded politely with a broad smile. "Thank you, Miss Skye. Your song has been the highlight of the evening."

"Indeed, it has," said Alasdair. "Shall we retire to the drawing room for pipe and a dram of whisky?"

Glenlyon stood, rubbing his skeletal fingers. "That and a round of cards."

All of the men followed suit, ignoring Skye and moving out the door. All but Kier. He strode up to her and gave a polite bow. "Have you an escort home, miss?"

She looked for Hugh, but he'd also left with the others. "No, but I'm afraid my parents would be furious if you walked me home, Lieutenant."

"Aye, well, I'll not allow you to go alone, especially not when the troops have liquored up in the brewhouse."

Again she looked beyond him. "Will you not be missed?"

He batted his hand through the air. "Not by Glenlyon, though Hugh MacIain might have something to say come morning."

"I can go back to the kitchen and see if someone there might be so kind."

He offered his elbow. "Come. Besides, I wanted us to part on more pleasant terms."

She didn't take it. "Part? Have you received news as to your deployment?"

"Not yet, but Glenlyon expects a missive any day now."

He tapped her shoulder, urging her forward but Skye held up her finger. "I almost forgot." She reached into her pocket. "I found this whilst sweeping the floor."

"Ma's miniature." He grinned. "I thought it was lost."

"You wouldn't want to lose a keepsake such as that."

"Thank you." He gestured toward the door. "Let us make haste afore someone decides that having a Campbell escort a MacIain lass home is a sacrilege."

Outside, a blast of frigid air made Skye shiver. "Heavens, I'll be happy when spring comes."

"I think we all will." He removed his cloak. "Here. Wear this."

"No need." She hastened toward the weaver's shop. "I'll borrow an extra blanket."

"Isn't it locked?"

"What on earth for?"

"Something could be stolen."

"From the laird? Mayhap on Campbell lands, but I assure you, a MacIain would never steal from a MacIain."

Kier chuckled. "I'll take your word for it."

Skye opened the door and stepped inside while warmth enveloped her. "The coals are still bright in the hearth." A crackle of anticipation coursed across her skin as he moved behind her. His aura made her shiver even though it wasn't cold inside. Oh no, she didn't need to turn around to feel his looming presence.

"Then we shan't need to light a candle."

"The blankets are over here." Again he followed and as Skye reached for a blanket, his hand slipped to her waist.

"I've missed you," he said, his deep voice rumbling through her entire body.

"I've missed you as well." She clutched a blanket to her chest, trying to breathe. "The past few days have been torturous."

"They have." Out of the corner of her eye, she saw him dip his head. His warm breath skimmed her neck right before he kissed her. Light, feathery kisses trailed across her nape while his strong hands slid around her waist. "Why is it I cannot stop myself from thinking of you every waking hour?"

"You, as well?" she asked breathlessly.

"Dear God, bonny Skye. I am tortured by your beauty, by your kindness and your strength of spirit. Ever since I walked away from your cottage, I have thought of nothing else but you."

Closing her eyes. Skye dropped the blanket and clutched her hands atop his arms. "What is it between us?"

"I only know that I have never felt like this before."

"Nor I."

She let him turn her around and pull her into his embrace. He claimed her mouth with deep, wondrous swirls of his tongue. Melting into him, Skye greedily returned his kiss, sliding her hands to his back and clinging to him for her very life. His chest molded to her breasts, his hips to her hips, making a hot yearning deep inside blast into an unquenchable fire. She met him rub for rub, yet it wasn't enough.

Kier's hands slid down and gripped her buttocks. Lord Almighty, the pressure rose. Skye moved with his friction. His hands were magical, every touch bringing a new sensation. His lips trailed down to her bodice as he released the tie and exposed her stays. Dipping his finger below the boning, Skye cried out when he brushed her nipple. And then his lips were on her with such passion, all she could think about was shamelessly exposing her breasts to him.

"What is happening to me?" she asked.

"Don't think, just feel."

Chapter Eight

Last eve, it had taken Kier more self-control than he'd ever exerted in his life to stop kissing Skye and walk her home. On the following morn, Captain Glenlyon had sent Kier on an errand to take the rope ferry across the wintry swells of Loch Leven and deliver a missive to Major Duncanson's headquarters in North Ballachulish. Now on his return journey, he planned to intercept Skye on her way home from the weaver's shop and apologize for taking liberties, but the blasted captain saw him first.

"Nephew!" Glenlyon hollered, cantering his enormous black Norfolk Trotter across the courtyard whilst holding his in place to combat the icy sideways wind. "Did the major send his reply with you?"

Kier reined his garron pony to a stop. "Unfortunately no, sir."

"Blast. I fear we'll be stuck in this abominable hell hole for the rest of our days." He signaled with a flick of his fingers. "Come, you shall dine with me at Brody MacDonald's house in Inverrigan this eve, then we'll have a game of cards with the Old Fox's sons, the bastards."

"Beg your pardon, sir, but if you abhor them so much then why are you playacting at being so amenable?" Kier took a forlorn look at the weaver's shop as they rode past. Snow had started to fall and marred his vision. Nonetheless, Skye was nowhere near either window.

"Colonel Hill's directive was to be neighborly whilst I analyze as to whether Alasdair will stand beside his oath of fealty to King William."

"And your opinion?" asked Kier.

"Does a man change his ways after sixty years of reiving just because he signs his name to a piece of parchment?"

"I think he can if given the right motivation."

"Are you referring to the money promised by the Earl of Breadalbane?"

Kier nodded. "Mostly."

"You ken as well as I, William's coffers have been bled by the war in Flanders. There's not a Highland chief who'll see a farthing, including me or your da."

"Aye, but Uncle Breadalbane wasn't daft enough to make empty promises to the likes of us."

By the time they arrived at Brody MacDonald's house, the weather had grown worse and an inch of snow had fallen.

Kier pulled the collar of his mantle closed tight. "I'll stable the horses."

"My thanks. I'll be in my chamber above stairs dressing for dinner."

Kier took the reins and headed for the stable. At least the captain had a chamber of his own. Privacy was the one thing the lieutenant missed the most from home.

After a meal of roast pheasant with their host, a couple of Glenlyon's officers and Sandy MacIain, Hugh arrived with his brother, Og.

Already liquored up and red in the nose, Glenlyon himself answered the door. A gust of wind blew in a flurry of snow. "Gentlemen, the cards are waiting."

Stepping inside, Hugh raised a flagon of whisky. "From my still in the hills. The spring water there adds flavor that cannot be surpassed. The spirit slides over the tongue like nectar."

Glenlyon took the bottle and slapped the MacIain heir on the back. "You're a man of good taste."

Sitting beside Cuthbert Hunter, Sandy waved from the table. "Brothers, come and save me from this shark—he's winning already."

"What? You didn't wait for us?" asked Og.

"Just a wee wager," Glenlyon said, handing the whisky bottle to Brody. "Drams all round, if you please."

Hugh pulled up a seat. "Better you than I, little brother."

Glenlyon shuffled the deck with his long, gnarled fingers. "Shall we play All Fours?"

"Very well." Hugh arched his brow at Og. "Why not make three teams of pairs to mix it up a bit?"

The captain grinned. "I'm not overly fond of splitting my winnings."

"Who says you'll win?" grumbled Og. Of all the MacIains, Kier trusted the middle son the least. Og was the only one of Alasdair's sons who'd made it clear the presence of the regiment was unwelcomed. And his steely-eyed glare sweeping across the faces confirmed the man's slant.

"Come, Uncle." Sandy raised his cup. "Side with me and we'll show this lot of rabble how skilled we are."

Glenlyon lowered his gaze to his hands as he shuffled the deck one more time. "Three pairs it is. I'll play with Sandy—Hunter and Hugh—Brody and Og. Kier, you're the arbitrator. Let no man accuse the other of foul play." He threw his head back with a hearty laugh. "I'm feeling lucky this eve."

Kier leaned back in his chair and stretched out his legs, crossing them at the ankles. It was always a relief not to have to gamble against his uncle. Especially when Glenlyon lost.

The man would give away his youngest daughter if it meant he'd take home the kitty.

Hugh reached in his sporran and pulled out a handful of coins, slapping them onto the table. "Then let's have at it. When this pile is gone, I'm heading to my bed. There's a storm brewing and I'd prefer not to sleep under Brody's table."

"Me as well," said Og. "In the past fortnight I've had enough to drink to keep my head swimming until spring."

Cuthbert snorted. "I've never seen anyone match the captain like you MacIain lads."

Og raised his cup. "Had a good teacher."

"Och aye," agreed Glenlyon. "Your da can put it away for certain. I'll be dining with him in the manse again on the morrow."

Hugh took a sip of whisky. "You wouldn't want to miss any table prepared by Ma. She's even pulled the rhubarb from the cellar for a tart."

Glenlyon rubbed his belly. "I'll look forward to such a feast with great anticipation." He sipped his whisky, then his rheumy eyes popped. "Mm. You distilled this yourself?"

Hugh nodded. "Aye. A man needs a great many talents to survive in these times."

The captain dealt the first round. "Many talents, indeed."

Kier nursed his whisky while he watched one team to the next deal the cards. Not surprisingly, Hugh was lucky. Glenlyon and Sandy were not. All the while, the captain's nose grew redder while his eyes drooped further. Until Brody answered a demanding knock at the door.

"Captain Drummond with a missive for Captain Campbell."

The Captain delivering the missive? Must be important for certain.

Kier glanced around the host and regarded Drummond, Major Duncanson's officer. Bloody hell, if the major had a reply so soon, why hadn't he retained Kier in Ballachulish? *Typical of the army.* "They sent you out in this weather?"

Moving inside, Drummond shot Kier a leer as he handed the missive to Glenlyon.

Across the table, Hugh brushed his fingers over the hilt of his dirk. Og ground his fist into his palm. Sandy set his cards down and slipped his hand into his sleeve.

The hair on the back of Kier's neck stood on end as his every muscle tensed. Holding his breath, he sat forward and watched while the captain slid his finger under the red wax seal and read. Brody stood beside Drummond without offering the officer a seat or a tot of whisky.

Glenlyon arched a single eyebrow as he folded the missive and stashed it in his waistcoat. Looking up, he grinned. "At long last my orders have arrived." He looked to Brody and stood. "The burden we've put on Clan Iain Abrach has been lifted, but I've much to attend to afore the sun rises on the morrow."

Every man stood and Hugh extended his hand. "It has been our pleasure to receive you and your men as guests."

"Aye," the captain said sounding completely in his cups. Glenlyon shook Hugh's hand, though his gaze wandered sideways. "Thank you for your generous hospitality. My only regret is I haven't relieved you of that pile of coin yet this eve."

After the MacIain men took their leave, the captain sobered as if the closing of the door brought an elixir of sobriety. "Gather the troops, men. We've much to plan afore daybreak."

***

Assembled in Brody MacDonald's barn, Kier stood at the front of the regiment in complete and utter disbelief at the orders he'd just heard. Dear God, he was a soldier of the crown, but never in his life had he wanted to mutiny as much as he did right now.

His chest tightened while his hands shook.

Put all to the sword under seventy? Take special care that the Old Fox and his sons do not survive? Secure all avenues to ensure no man survives?

Jesus Christ, King William was asking them to commit genocide.

Glenlyon folded his orders and stuffed them into his coat as he started back to the house.

"Captain, sir." Kier hastened after him with Lindsay and Cuthbert in his wake. "May I please see the order?"

Glenlyon stopped and narrowed his gaze. "You question my authority?"

"Not at all, sir." Kier clenched his fists behind his back, determined to stop this madness. "It's hard to believe. I'm nothing short of shocked and merely ask to see it for myself."

"Will that change anything? Our orders have come. We have a grave task to perform come five o'clock, and I suggest you ready your weapons."

Kier blocked his uncle's path and stood firm. "This is an abomination and you ken it. You ken it in your very beard!"

Glenlyon sauntered forward, shoving his finger into Kier's chest. "How dare you question the motives of the king, you sniveling whelp? You are but a lowly lieutenant, paid to serve and carry out His Majesty's bidding even if you are my nephew."

Kier wasn't about to back down. "But we've accepted the MacIain's hospitality. Turning around and murdering them in cold blood goes against the very fiber of Highland values that has been passed down from our forefathers and those who came afore them!"

Glenlyon sniffed with an ugly scowl. "Are you telling me you're not man enough to follow through with your sworn duty? This is not a gathering. This is bloody war."

Kier stretched to his full height, making the captain crane his neck. "This is the mass extermination of a clan and you ken it. You ken right down to your gambling, debauching heart."

"I am a soldier and I will do my king's bidding." With a thrust of his hand, Glenlyon motioned to Lindsay. "Seize him!"

A moment too late to flee, Kier bucked as Lindsay and Hunter clamped their fingers tight around his arms. "Seize me for speaking with a modicum of sanity?"

Hemp rope bit as it wound around his wrists.

"I kent you were smitten with that songbird as soon as she opened her mouth last eve. And then Lindsay confirmed it. He reported that he saw you taking the lass into the weaver's shop. Did you think for one moment why I sent you on an errand this day? What would it have done to my plans if the lassie's father had riled the Old Fox? The bastards could have taken up arms."

Kier twisted and fought his captors. "You kent about this all along? Good God, you're a cold-blooded murderer!"

"MacIain's time has come and I'm the deliverer of his salvation. I'll dirk every bloody savage myself if I have to, including your bonny wench." Glenlyon slapped his hand through the air. "Take this this yellow turncoat from my sight and throw him in the woodshed. Let it be known if any dragoon tries to foil our plans, I shall personally preside over his hanging!"

Chapter Nine

Shivering in the bitter cold, Kier's wrists rubbed raw as he fought to twist from his bindings. He'd put up a fight when Lindsay and Cuthbert tried to haul him away and it had taken six dragoons to hogtie him. They gave him a half-dozen kicks to the ribs for good measure as well. His own damned men, for God's sakes.

Now he lay face down with his wrists bound to his ankles with but a foot of rope between them. His arms cramped, his back felt like he'd been stabbed and breathing caused shooting pains to his ribs. He'd hollered until his throat was sore. No one was coming. The lot of them were either mindless sheep or completely mad.

Frantic to free himself, Kier arched up, bearing his cramping muscles, stretching to reach the rope around his ankles. His trembling fingers brushed the knots as he searched an end piece. Damnation, the bastards hadn't given him a chance. What in God's name were they thinking? And one of them had been Nicoll—his most trusted sentinel. Didn't anyone see the madness of their orders? Didn't anyone give a rat's arse about the clansmen who'd taken them into their homes and fed them for a fortnight?

Footsteps crunched the snow outside.

"You there," Kier yelled. "Help!"

A wee lad about Tommy's age stepped into the woodshed holding a lantern. "Lieutenant Campbell?"

"One and the same, lad. Haste. Cut these binds. A great calamity is about to unfold."

The boy set the lantern on the ground. "What kind of calamity?"

"Cut this rope and I'll tell you all."

"Who did this?"

"Glenlyon."

The boy stood near the door, wringing his hands as if Kier might spring up and attack. "What did you do?"

"For the love of God, untie me!"

"Och, you do not have to yell." The lad knelt and pulled his eating knife from his hose.

Kier breathed a sigh of relief when he started sawing. "What is your name?"

"Malcolm."

"Thank you, son. I'm in your debt." The rope began to ease and Kier pulled against it. "Tell me, what are you doing up at this hour?"

"'Tis my job to see to it the master's fire is lit afore daybreak."

"Is that Brody MacDonald?"

"Aye, sir."

"Pray, what is the hour?"

"Near enough to five, sir."

"Jesus Christ." The rope snapped. Kier rolled to his arse and shoved the bindings from his hands and ankles. Then he grasped the lad by the shoulders. "Glenlyon's orders are to massacre the entire clan—put all under seventy to fire and sword. Run now and sound the alarm. Tell them…tell them to haste south. That's the only pass not guarded by troops."

"But—"

Musket shots boomed from across the river.

Kier gave Malcolm a shove. "Haste ye as fast as your legs can run—and stay away from the soldiers lest you end up with a musket ball in your heart!"

The lad kicked the lantern as he ran from the shed. Fire whisked up the wood in a blink of an eye. Running for his horse, Kier didn't stop to give the flames a second look.

One thing consumed his mind.

Find Skye before some bastard took a dirk to her throat.

Chapter Ten

The sudden crack from a musket ripped Skye from deep sleep. Her heart flew to her throat with the next volley of gunfire. Beyond the cottage shouting rose across the Coe. Women shrieked and pleaded for mercy.

Sitting up, Skye clutched the bedclothes under her chin, praying the terror was a nightmare. But the ice coursing through her blood told her the terror was all too real. A raid had begun and soldiers were closing in. More shots rang in her ears.

"Burn them out!" a man yelled while horses whinnied.

Something thudded on the roof.

"Fire!" Tommy screamed.

Da burst from his box bed, dirk in hand. "I kent those backstabbers were turncoats. I read it in their eyes from the first instant they arrived."

Skye hurried down from her bed, coughing as smoke oozed from above. "What are we to do?"

Ma pulled blankets from the beds. "Haste! Put these around your shoulders." She shoved a plaid into Skye's arms. "Jimmy, you must carry our son."

The door burst open with a blast of icy air. Kier's fierce gaze swept past Skye's as he dashed to Tommy's pallet while clumps of snow showered in his wake. "Glenlyon's been ordered to put all under seventy under the knife. MacIain is dead. The bastards are burning you out!"

Da lunged with his dagger. "You're the cause of this, Campbell! I'll dirk you in the back—"

Whipping around, Kier caught Da's wrist, stopping the knife before it plunged into his flesh. "Jesus Christ, man. Can you not see I'm trying to help? I've a horse outside and I've just killed two of my men to save the likes of you!"

He shoved Da to the ground, the old man's expression contorted by disbelief and utter terror.

Ma pushed her feet into her boots. "Where are we to go?" she asked, her voice shrill.

Kier hoisted Tommy over his shoulder, blankets and all. "The southern pass is the only outlet not blocked by the army."

More musket fire blasted from outside. Shrieks and screams turned Skye's stomach.

"How do we escape?" she asked, following her mother's example and coughing while the smoke stung her eyes. "There's a foot or more of snow. They're murdering women. 'Tis a massacre!"

Kier stopped at the door, his expression dark. "It is. We keep off the trail. Tommy and Mistress Sineag can ride my horse. The two dragoons sent to burn you out are dead, but there'll be more. Anyone who stays in the Coe will be mercilessly cut down." He cracked open the door and peeked outside. "We stay together. Follow me."

"I cannot believe I'm trusting a bloody Campbell," Da grumbled under his breath.

"Merciful Father," Skye whispered, tiptoeing on Kier's heels into the darkness lit by the blaze on the cottage roof. If there were time, she'd tell her father exactly how daft he sounded. But right now each and every one of them had to stay alive.

Kier hoisted Tommy to the saddle and handed up his musket, powder horn and a pouch of lead balls. "I taught you how to use this lad. Load it now. If a redcoat steps in your path, shoot him afore he kills you."

The lad's eyes grew as round as silver guineas, but he took the weapon. "Aye, sir."

Da hastened to help Ma mount behind the lad. Once aboard, she crossed herself while another volley of gunfire came from Cameron MacDonald's croft across the paddock. "God save us."

At a jog, Kier headed for the river following the trail he must have cut through the snow on his way in. "The drifts are not as deep along the shore. And if we keep to the trees, we'll not be spotted."

"'Tis a bloody whiteout," Da said, struggling to keep pace. "No one will be able to see us once we reach the trees."

"Agreed," Kier said over his shoulder.

Gasping, Skye stumbled face-first into a drift. Kier grabbed her by the elbow and pulled her up. "Can you walk, lass?"

"Aye," she said, her teeth chattering. "The snow is caking around the hem of my skirts."

"I'll carry you, then." In the blink of an eye, he swept her into his arms and darted for the shelter of the trees.

"Halt!" A menacing voice shouted behind them.

"Tommy, shoot!" bellowed Kier, setting Skye on her feet.

The musket blasted but Tommy missed. With a hiss of the blade, Kier drew his sword, but Da pulled his dagger from his sleeve and threw it into the dragoon's heart.

Sentinel Dyatt clutched at the knife's hilt, dropped to his knees and fell face-first to the snow.

Kier sheathed his weapon. "There'll be more, mark me."

"Then I'll retrieve my dagger," said Da. "Go on. I'll meet you at the river."

***

The bloody snow continued to impede their progress while Kier led Skye's bedraggled family into the hills. Daylight arrived nearly two hours after the shooting began and, by that time, they'd climbed well into the foothills leading to *Meall Mòr*. That morning Kier had glimpsed a few others running for their lives, some in their nightshirts, their feet bare. Every face he saw was filled with terror, shocked and panic stricken.

No one dared travel with them. They took one look at Kier still dressed in a government uniform and they ran.

He'd endured cold and misery before, but only a madman would set out in this weather, let alone with a wounded child, two women and a man well past his prime. But they were the fortunate ones. Mistress Sineag had the forethought to bring blankets and everyone aside from Tommy was wearing boots. They even had a horse.

The poor survivors, who ran for their lives wearing nothing but a nightshirt whilst under fire and sword, mightn't make it through the day. Not if the wrath of God didn't ease.

But the blizzard did turn to tiny flakes of snow as they climbed further into the mountains. The midday sun didn't make an appearance, though the cloud cover brightened. Kier crossed a path, showing footprints nearly hidden by freshly fallen snow. He followed it into the pass.

"The *Meall Mòr* shielings are up this way," said Jimmy. "We'll find shelter up there."

"It appears as if some of the survivors are heading that way as well," Kier said.

An hour later, they stopped outside a shieling, smoke rising from its thatch and the snow trampled around the exterior.

Jimmy strode forward and threw back his shoulders. "I'll go in first. If they see your coat, they'll likely run you through afore you have a chance to cry for help."

"Very well." Kier helped Mistress Sineag to dismount, then pulled Tommy into his arms.

Skye moved beside him. "Mayhap you should remove your coat."

"And freeze to death? They all ken who I am."

"Hello, inside! Jimmy of Clan Iain Abrach here."

"Wait with your hands up," came the reply.

"Tis Og," said Skye. "He's hotter than a firebrand, that one."

Kier inclined his lips toward her ear. "I ken Og well and 'tis a good thing Hugh was the firstborn."

"If he survived," Sineag mumbled beside them.

When the door opened, Og's gaze immediately shifted from Jimmy to Kier. "Ye bloody murderer!" He marched forward, sword at the ready.

"Move!" Shoving Tommy into Skye's arms and pushing them away, Kier drew his sword just as the MacIain man attacked with a downward strike to the head. As Kier raised his blade to defend himself, iron met iron with a deafening clang. His arms nearly gave way. God's bones, he'd been awake all night fighting his bindings. He rescued Skye and her kin before they succumbed to Glenlyon's wrath. He'd climbed the mountains of Glencoe on foot, trudging through three-foot drifts of snow. His legs felt weighed down by seven stone weights and, rather than being heralded a hero, he was fighting for his life.

Og attacked with brutal animosity, like a man gone wild.

Somewhere in the back of his mind, Skye's screams registered. Kier deflected every vicious strike from the behemoth, who hacked with vengeance as if he'd saved up his ire and aimed to make Kier pay. Backed into a wall of rock,

Kier prayed the lass was safe. He couldn't shift his eyes from the madman or his heart was sure to meet with cold steel.

Og lunged with a slice to the throat. Kier ducked under. After spinning away, he regained a defensive stance. "I don't want to fight you."

"I don't give a rat's arse what you want!" Rage filled Og's eyes as he attacked, going for the kill.

Kier jumped aside and smashed the hilt of his weapon into the man's hand. Og bellowed in pain as his sword fell to the ground. Diving for the hilt, Kier plucked the blade from the snow and rolled sideways with enough momentum to rise to his feet.

Holding his hands steady, Kier trained both swords on the madman. "I am *not* your enemy."

"No? You're a Campbell. You wear the red coat. Your bloody *uncle* just killed my father. My mother's in there bleeding to death from her..." Og dropped to his knees, tears streaming down his cheeks. "Your murdering kin violated her with a dagger."

Kier lowered the swords, his gut turning over with sickly bile. Never in his life had he seen such insanity.

"Og, go inside." Hugh MacIain marched toward them with Jimmy in his wake.

Kier searched for Skye. She was crying with her face in her hands while, beside her, the matron provided a crutch for Tommy.

In a show of trust, Kier handed the hilt of Og's sword to Hugh. "I have no words to express the revulsion I harbor for this day's events."

The man looked crushed, yet ire flashed through his eyes. "Events you call them?"

Kier pursed his lips. There would be no placating these people. They had been wronged by his own kin, by the government army he'd thought he loved.

Hugh shoved the sword into the snow. "Jimmy told me you saved his family—let the wounded lad and his mother ride your horse. I thank you for that."

Looking the man in the eye, Kier gave a nod while the snow turned their cloaks white.

MacIain nodded to the southern side of the pass. "But you cannot stay."

"I ken."

"You do not ken shite. I have twenty mouths in there to feed and God kens how many others will arrive afore nightfall. Every passing moment the snow grows deeper and I have nothing to feed them with aside from the meat from my horse."

Kier looked to his own mount with a twinge of guilt. If he left the beast here for the MacIains, he'd be dead by morning.

"You can move on. You're a Campbell. You'll not be shot if you show your face down below. But us? My father signed the oath of fealty to William of Orange and, yet, Glenlyon still murdered him." Hugh's eyes filled with rage as his Adam's apple bobbed. "We brought you into our homes. We showed those brutal savages nothing but genuine Highland hospitality and they butchered us for it!"

Kier stood there for a moment, his feet freezing in the snow. Skye looked up with pleading eyes, her lips trembling. "Stay," she mouthed.

"Would you allow me a moment to say farewell to Miss Skye?"

"What is the point of that?" asked her father. "Can you not see you've caused the lass enough consternation? She thinks she's in love with you."

Love?

Kier's heart twisted. If only he'd told her that he loved her. But now? When their very lives hung on a precipice? "Please," Kier asked pushing up his sleeves and showing his raw wrists. "Have I not shown my honor this day? If it weren't for a lad named Malcolm, I would still be tied up in Brody MacDonald's woodshed."

"Malcolm?" Hugh glanced back toward the shieling. "His father said if it weren't for the lad raising the alarm, they'd be dead as well."

Skye ran forward and flung her arms around Kier. "This man saved my family and if you turn him away I'll be going with him."

Kier clutched his arm tightly across her shoulders. "If she stays with me, I can protect her. She'll not starve. On that I give my word."

"But you are not married!" Mistress Sineag hastened forward.

Skye tightened her grip. "I'm going with Kier."

"I forbid it!" Jimmy grabbed his daughter's arm and yanked her away. "Your place is with Clan Iain Abrach, not with the backstabbing Campbells."

"But he saved us," Skye argued.

"Aye, one man in a clan who doesn't have a black heart. The rest are Satan's spawn. Nay, lassie. The lieutenant is not for the likes of you."

Skye twisted her arm, trying to escape. "Kier, please!"

Lunging, he reached for her.

"I forbid it," boomed Hugh, shoving between them. "I am clan chief now and my word is law on these lands."

Kier dropped his hands. Mayhap the men were right. She'd be better off with her own kin. He was a Campbell, a scourge in the eyes of these people. God save him, if it was right to let her go, why did Kier feel like Hugh had ripped his heart out of his chest?

Jimmy dragged the lass into the shieling. Skye's muffled protests rose through the snow-covered thatch.

"Go on, now." MacIain thrust his finger toward the horse. "Because you helped Jimmy to safety, I'll let you walk away this once. But if you ever cross my path again, I'll not be so lenient."

Kier started for his mount. "I said it afore. You ken I'd take care of the lass."

"Would you marry her?"

He stopped and gave Hugh a sober stare. "Aye."

"Even if your father forbade it?"

"Even then."

Hugh said nothing and ushered the rest of Skye's family inside, leaving Kier alone knee-deep in snow. The lieutenant who had gone against an order from the king to save the woman who stirred his blood like no other, stared at the door of the shieling, his blood running hot. "Skyyyyyyye!" he bellowed.

Never in his life had he felt so strongly about anything. If he mounted his horse and left without her, he could very well be signing her death decree. God save him, she would not be left to suffer. Twenty or more people trying to survive the winter in a tumbledown shack? He yanked open the door, strode inside, collected the lass in his arms and marched for his horse.

Chapter Eleven

Skye curled against Kier's chest while the horse trudged through the snow. Though wrapped in a blanket, she was colder than she'd ever been in her life. Flurries continued throughout the arduous journey through the glens. Clouds settled on the white cliffs above as if they planned to stay and dump an endless shower of snow, impeding their progress until the pony could move no more.

Overcome with the day's events, a hollow void filled her chest. She closed her eyes and thanked God for Kier. But the catastrophe at *Meall Mòr* had taken a horrific and devastating trauma and made it worse. Kier had turned against his clan to help her and, in return, her kin had repaid him with nothing but rebuff.

They were a pair of outcasts in a land gone mad.

Kier brushed the snow from her shoulder. "Are you all right?"

"Alive. Shocked."

His warm breath skimmed her skin as he pressed his lips to her forehead. "I reckon we all are stunned."

"Where are we heading?"

"Loch Dochart. I pray my da will take us in."

"And if not?"

"Mayhap we should go to Glasgow and sail for the Americas."

"Leave my family? My home..." She shuddered. *What home?*

Kier's lips formed a thin line, his eyes taking on a hard stare. "This is no time to be planning for the future. We'll need shelter afore nightfall."

"Aye." Skye swiped a hand across her face. "I feel awful about leaving my family up there in that shieling with nothing..."

"Hugh will protect them. He's a good man."

"He's your enemy."

"That doesn't mean I disrespect him. Besides, at the moment, I cannot afford to claim any man as my enemy...a...aside from Glenlyon."

Skye shuddered. "I'm glad of it."

"I suppose I am as well."

"Do you think my kin will ever forgive me?"

"There's nothing to forgive, lass. Your parents will love you in their hearts no matter what."

Another shiver coursed over her skin. She didn't feel loved. In fact, aside from the Highlander cradling her in his arms, she felt lost, exiled—like a tinker without a home.

Melancholy spread a black emptiness from her heart through her limbs. Again they rode in silence while God continued to douse them with snow. Their march grew slower and slower until Kier pulled the horse to a halt outside an abandoned shieling.

"Where are we?" Skye asked.

"Dalness—a hunting shelter used by my clan. We can weather the night here." Kier dismounted then helped her down. He had to clear away the snow to wedge open the door. He found a candle and lit it by striking flint to his dirk.

Rubbing the outside of her arms, Skye turned full circle—there was a table and an old straw mattress on a rope frame with a fire pit at one end. "'Tis better than freezing to death in the snow."

"There should be some wood stacked along the south side. Do you think you can manage lighting a fire whilst I hunt us something to eat?"

"Aye." Skye nodded as her stomach growled. She hadn't eaten since last eve. With the excitement, she hadn't even thought about food, but now her hands started to shake for the hunger.

By the time Kier returned, Skye had a fire going and her fingers had thawed from clearing snow off the thatch to allow the smoke to escape. Huddled beside the flames, she stood while Kier closed the rickety door and held up a skinned hare. "This will provide a good meal."

She breathed a sigh of relief. "I was afraid you wouldn't be able to find a thing in this weather."

"Mayhap our luck has turned for the better." He grinned then set to using a length of rope to suspend the carcass over the fire.

"You've done this afore."

"Many times."

"Do you like hunting?"

"For the most part. Just not knee-deep in snow."

She resumed her seat, folding her legs and patting the place beside her. "You'd best sit by the fire whist the rabbit cooks."

"I won't argue." He joined her and removed his gloves, setting them by the rocks to dry.

"How far are we from Loch Dochart?" she asked.

"About thirty miles if we stick to the glens. In this weather, we'd best start at first light on the morrow and pray we make it by dusk." Kier stretched then wrapped an arm around her shoulder and encouraged her to rest against him.

"Will your pony withstand the journey?" she asked, closing her eyes and savoring his closeness.

"I think so. He's a tough old garron. I led him down to the burn—he has the shelter of the trees, and the water is still running there—a bit of grass is showing as well."

"Thank heavens."

They sat together in each other's embrace, staring into the flames of the fire. Too much had changed since last eve. Too many horrors had happened to even begin to think about. And worse, as fugitives, who knew what the morrow might bring?

The only thing Skye allowed herself to think about was the man beside her. If he had not come to her cottage that morn, she and her kin would be dead with the other ill-fated souls in Glencoe.

I owe him my life.

Not long and the juices from the rabbit dripped to the flames, making them leap and hiss. The smell served to heighten Skye's hunger. By the time Kier cut off a slice of meat and handed it to her, she ate greedily, stuffing her mouth as if she had been starved for sennights.

They gorged themselves on rabbit and drank from Kier's flask. Finally, he pointed to the two remaining legs. "Mayhap we should save a bit for the morn. I don't imagine we'll find much else afore we reach Sigurd Castle."

Skye agreed and they sat together for a time while Kier gently rocked her, his hand caressing. Dear God, Skye wanted to belong to him, to be a part of something and not hanging from a precipice, not knowing what ills the morrow would bring. "Inside the shieling I-I heard you talking to Hugh. Did you mean what you said?" she asked, curling over a bit, afraid his reply might cut her to the quick.

"Aye. Every word." With the crook of his finger he inclined her chin upward. "I ken we've only known each other for a very short time, but from the first day I saw you standing in the upstairs window of the weaver's shop, you've stirred my blood."

"Do you love me?"

"With my very being."

Her heart fluttered. "And you would marry me?"

"Aye, I said it to Hugh, and I swear it to you now."

She didn't tremble at all as she stood, dropping the arisaid from her shoulders. There had been no time to don a kirtle or socks or a set of stays. It took but a blink of an eye to slip out of her boots and pull her shift over her head.

Kier watched her every move, his eyes growing dark and filling with desire. His breathing became labored as he rose to his feet. "I will marry you the Highland way this eve, if you agree to be my wife."

Standing naked before him, Skye swallowed against the thickening in her throat. She knew of the ancient Highland rite of marriage when a lass consents for a man to take her. She knew what he was asking of her. It meant she would lay with him and they would be married in the eyes of clan and kin.

She didn't blink as she met his gaze. "It would be an honor to serve the man who risked everything to save my family from the bane of fire and sword this very morn."

His coat dropped to the floor as he stared into her eyes. His boots slipped off. Skye could scarcely breathe as his hand moved to his belt. With a flick of his wrist, his weapons dropped to the ground. Stepping in, she unpinned the brooch at his shoulder and pulled the length of tartan away, unwrapping it from his hips until it billowed to the floor. With a sultry grin, he pulled his shirt over his head and cast it aside.

Bare as God intended, he stood before her. His body had not an ounce of fat—a powerful chest, supported by a rippling abdomen, but what truly took her breath away was the full length of virile manhood jutting from a nest of black curls.

Skye gasped, tapping her lips with the tips of her fingers. "You are magnificent."

He chuckled, stepping in and grasping her hands. "Let me look at you." She eased the tension in her arms as he spread them wide. "I have never seen a sight more beautiful."

He pulled her into his arms and covered her mouth with a kiss filled with fire, a kiss like he wanted to devour her. As his hot flesh rubbed hers, the intense pull of longing shot between her legs. She clutched him tighter, craving more, craving to be joined with him.

Kier lifted her into his arms. "Wrap your legs around me."

Doing so made her entire body quake with delicious shudders as her slick core slid down his length. "What wizardry do you possess over me?" she asked with a gasp.

"'Tis the magic of passion between a man and a woman," he growled in her ear, carrying her to the bed and laying her atop a blanket.

Kier scarcely made it to the bed before he exploded. He'd thought Skye was the bonniest woman in the Highlands prior to seeing her naked, but now he knew in the depths of his soul she was the finest woman in all of Christendom. And she was his. Laying her on her back, Skye's tresses swarmed around her, making her look like a flesh and blood goddess.

On his knees, he pushed between her thighs and moved her hands to his rock-hard erection. "I want you to touch me."

Her lips parted as she stared at him, the corners of her mouth turning up. She stroked him with silken fingers while he shuddered with his mounting desire. "I want to please you. Show me how."

Seed leaked from the tip of his cock and he sucked in a sharp breath, clenching his arse cheeks to regain control. "Good God, no sweeter words have ever been spoke." No matter how much Kier desired to take her, to plunge inside heaven and soar to the stars, he had to make it right. "Tell me you will marry me."

"I will," she said breathlessly.

He thrust his hips forward as she began to milk him. But before he gave in to his need, he must seal their bond. "Will you hold me dear in your heart for the rest of your days?"

"I will cherish you forever."

His heart soared. "And I will be your husband. I promise to provide for you, to care for you, to love you and our bairns to come."

Kier lowered himself over bonny Skye as he kissed her, all of her. He trailed lips down her neck and buried his face between the mounds of her breasts. He suckled her nipples until she gasped and arched against him.

Chuckling, he rocked forward and brushed his cock along her exposed, swollen womanhood. She was so wet and hot, he nearly exploded. Staring up at him with the bonniest bluebell eyes, a look of pure passion filled Skye's expression as her breathing sped and her hips swirled against him.

Taking a stuttered inhale, Kier moved lower and shifted the tip of his cock to her opening. "Are ye ready to become my Highland bride?"

Skye quavered beneath him and nodded. "Aye, aye, aye!" Her parted lips, ruby red with passion, drove him to the brink of madness. He could wait no longer.

Gradually inching inside he held still, biting his lip. Holy hellfire, she was tighter than a new scabbard.

"Kier," she gasped, tensing beneath him.

"Am I hurting you?"

"A little." She shook her head. "Nay. It feels inexplicably good."

"Then guide me so I'll not cause you pain, *mo leannan*."

Nodding, her eyes filling with trust, she sank her lithe fingers into his buttocks and tugged. She let out a sharp gasp while she dictated the torturous pace. Kier fought to maintain control as this sensuous woman milked him, surrounded him, tight and wet. Skye strengthened her grip and swirled her hips until he reached the wall of her womb. Arching her back, her moans started low then came rapid and swift, sending him into a maelstrom of driving need. Kier could hold back no more. He drove into her again and again, the tight rippling of her walls taking him beyond the point of pure magic. Throwing back his head, he roared with his release.

Skye's hips met his thrusts. As he exploded, she arched up and cried out.

Panting, he rested on his elbows and gazed into the luminous pools of her eyes, so clear, he could glimpse into her soul. "God help me, I love you with every thread of my being."

Smiling like an angel, her hair damp from exertion, she caressed his face and drew his lips to hers. "I love you, Kier Campbell."

Kissing his bride, he swore he would never again let her go. He vowed to hold her in his embrace and protect her forever. Skye of Clan Iain Abrach was his.

Chapter Twelve

The weather and all of Christendom seemed against them as they headed to Sigurd Castle. Thank God Kier could traverse these lands in his sleep, because no sane man would be out in the sleet and snow and whipping wind unless he was running for his life.

They made it to the stables beside Loch Dochart well past dark and there wasn't a stable hand in sight. After tending to his horse and giving the garron a double ration of oats, Kier led Skye to the pier and helped her board a skiff used to ferry people to the tower house built by his ancestors atop a rocky isle.

Shivering, she blew on her fingers and panned her gaze up the looming old keep as he rowed. "It looks enormous, but brooding almost as if it's abandoned."

"'Tis the weather. Come spring when the bluebells and primrose are in bloom, 'tis not so stark."

"I've never been inside a castle afore." She cringed while her teeth chattered.

"It isn't much different from MacIain's manse."

With that, Skye's face fell. Kier didn't have to ask why. The shock of yesterday morn's events still stewed in his chest like boiling tar.

"Do you think your father will like me?" she asked.

"Aye." Kier knew Da would be difficult, but he would grow to love Skye in time.

Finn, the valet, met them at the enormous oak door. "Master Kier, whatever are you doing out in this weather? I reckon nary a fox has crawled from his hole for near on two days."

Kier embraced the faithful old servant. "Have you heard the news from Glencoe?"

"Nothing recent." The man looked to Skye and a shadow crossed his face. "Something grave has happened, has it not?"

"I'm afraid so, my friend. An act nothing short of genocide, led by Glenlyon."

"Dear God."

After introducing Skye, Kier explained about the rescue of her family and skirted around the details of his hasty marriage. "Would you please show Mistress Skye to my chamber and send up a tray of food and ale?"

She glanced at him with wide eyes. "You're not going with me?"

"I must have a word with my father alone first." He gestured toward the stairwell. "I'll join you anon."

Finn bowed. "Your da is in his solar, sir."

"I thought as much." Kier bowed in return and waited until the patter of their footsteps on the ancient sandstone stairs disappeared, then he dashed upward to the second floor.

When he entered the solar, Da lowered his gazette and looked up in surprise. In the past year, Father's hair had gone grayer, his face gaunter. "Kier? What the devil are you doing here? It has been blizzarding for two days."

"I've a great deal to tell you." Kier met his father's eyes with a somber stare. They shook hands as they always did. Da believed it was a sign of weakness for a man to embrace another, even in private. "Finn said you haven't received a messenger in days."

"No. Not that any sane man would venture out in this weather. There must be three feet of snow on the ground. Why the devil did you risk riding in a blizzard? Were you not in Fort William?"

"Glencoe." Keir moved to the sideboard and poured a tot of whisky for them both. After taking a seat, he launched into a detailed explanation of his regiment's arrival in the Coe and all that ensued right up until they arrived at Sigurd Castle.

Da's bloodshot eyes grew redder and enraged. "You mean to tell me you have not only committed treason against your clan, you have gone and wedded a MacIain, the scourge of the Highlands?"

Kier shoved back his chair and rose to his feet, grinding his knuckles into the table. "After all I've said, you cannot tell me you support the annihilation of an entire clan."

Whisky spewed from Da's lips. "Good God, Son. Are you daft? Clan Iain Abrach is our greatest enemy. We have feuded with the MacIains and MacDonalds since the rise of the Lords of the Isles." He pushed from the table so hard, his chair clattered to the floorboards. "*You* have gone against an order of the king and, worse, you've brought a fugitive into my house?"

Taking a step back, Kier looked at his father in disbelief. "Do you not care what is right, what is honorable?"

"'Tis about time you learned that honor has nothing to do with protecting clan and kin." Da pounded his fist. "To survive in these times, a man must bear that which he cannot change and ensure he stands on the right side of every feud. And *if* that means taking up fire and sword to rid the lands of thieving tinkers, then I stand by it with all my heart and soul."

If only Kier could plant his knuckles in that proud face. After four and twenty years, he finally saw his father for a yellow-bellied hypocrite—all the Campbells for their hypocrisy.

Da thrust his finger toward the door. "I would not turn a dog out in this weather, but come morn, you will take that *bitch* and never set foot on my lands again!"

***

Skye knew something was wrong as soon as Kier walked into the chamber. And all along, she'd known his father wouldn't see reason. The laird was a Campbell, after all. "What happened?" she asked.

"We'll be leaving come first light."

"That bad?"

"Worse. I've lost my inheritance."

Skye looked from one tapestry to the next. Kier's chamber was more opulent than anything she'd ever imagined. "Because of me?"

"Nay, because of injustice and outdated parochial views of an old man who could not see reason if it were presented to him on a platter hewn of solid gold."

She hid her face in her hands as her heart twisted inside her chest. "'Tis all my fault. Forgive me for bringing this upon you."

"Och, lass. You are nay the one who penned the order to put a clan to fire and sword." He pulled her into his arms. Skye tried to push away, but he held her with fierce strength. "I am a wealthy man for loving you. We shall make our own dynasty, you and I."

"What are you saying?" She craned her neck to see his face. "You weren't serious about sailing for the Americas?"

"I was. I hear there's land for the taking and it matters not where you were born. What matters is how you live your life and the honor borne in your heart."

"But what of Tommy, Ma...Da?"

"Once we're settled, we can send for them."

Closing her eyes, Skye clung to her husband. She knew her parents would never leave the Highlands, not unless Hugh ordered it and that wasn't likely. What were her parents doing now and what must they think of her for leaving them in the mountains? Who knew when it would be safe to go back? Her home was destroyed and the contents burned.

She looked Kier in the eye and cupped his whiskered cheeks between her palms. "My place is with you now."

Chapter Thirteen

Kier stood on the pier at the Port of Glasgow while he and Skye waited for the skiff to ferry them to the galleon moored in the Firth of Clyde. They'd waited a fortnight for the ship to undergo repairs for the voyage and had stayed in a guest house on Bridge Street. It wasn't easy trying to keep a low profile once the news of the massacre filtered down from the Highlands.

Everyone had something to say about it. Kier had burned his army coat. Once they arrived in Glasgow, he'd commissioned a tailor to fashion him a new suit of clothes and three new gowns, undergarments and a cloak for Skye. He'd paid for everything in coin, careful not to let on that he was a Campbell. In fact, he shortened the name to Camp even for the ship's manifest.

Not far down the pier, a Highland galley dropped anchor and a tall, dapper gentleman alighted with an entourage in tow. All men in his retinue wore kilts and sporrans with dirk and sword. They reminded Kier of MacIains, of Camerons, of MacDonalds and of Campbells. Here in the lowlands, Highlanders looked the same regardless of their politics.

When he looked up, the man stopped dead in his tracks. At first he looked as if he might draw his sword, but then he narrowed his gaze and scratched his chin. "Kier Campbell is it?"

With the tenor of his voice, something rang in Kier's head while the memory of the Battle of Dunkeld came back full force. He'd met this man on the battlefield, watched him fight valiantly and watched him elude the government troops, leading his men northward back to the MacDonald lands in Skye.

His wife beside him grasped Kier's arm. "Do you ken this man?"

"Aye." Squaring his shoulders, he held out his hand. "Donald MacDonald, Baronet of Sleat, it is my pleasure."

"Chieftain of Clan Donald?" Skye whispered with awe filling her voice. Clan Iain Abrach paid fealty to this man and his infamous kin.

The baronet grinned. "I've heard a great deal about you in the past several days."

Kier glanced toward the galleon, praying the skiff was on its way, but the crew hadn't yet lowered the boat to the surf. The last thing he needed was for his wife to watch him die fighting off a mob of MacDonalds. "I have no quarrel with you, sir."

"I should hope not." MacDonald gave Skye a wink. "It seems your quarrel is with your own clan."

Kier pursed his lips.

But Skye stepped forward. "He saved me and my family from Glenlyon's sword."

MacDonald crossed his arms with a nod. "A wee lad named Malcolm said his family was spared due to Campbell's heroism as well. We suspect there might be a few dragoons pushing up daisies on account of him come spring."

Where is that goddamned skiff? Keir shot another look to the galleon.

Skye scurried forward and grasped the baronet's arm. "Please, sir. Have you word of my family? Are they safe?"

"Aye, safe with Hugh, still up at *Meall Mòr*. But they're living like dogs. I reckon it'll be a cold day in hell afore we bring the culprits to justice."

"The sooner the better," Kier mumbled.

Skye turned with a radiant smile. "They'll be all right. I ken they will."

The baronet seemed not to notice Skye's sudden joy and continued to look at Kier as if he posed a quandary. "You studied at University, did you not?"

"Aye. Edinburgh." Kier pulled Skye behind him and stepped forward. "Why do you ask?"

"I could use a man like you."

"I beg your pardon?"

"I've a proposition to make. Would you share my coach?"

Kier threw his thumb over his shoulder. "I'm afraid we have a ship to board as soon as the captain sends the skiff."

Sir Donald looked to the galleon. "Are you certain you want to sail to the Americas and risk your very lives to sickness or worse, a death in Davey Jones' locker?"

Skye grasped Kier's hand and squeezed. Could he trust this man? Kier gave MacDonald a somber stare. "What is your proposal, sir? Since you are aware of my actions in Glencoe, there is an army of men who'd sooner see me swinging by the hangman's noose, including my father."

"I need a learned man to embark upon a new salt pan operation in Trotternish on the Isle of Skye—lands tended by MacDonald kin. I have two caveats, however."

"And they would be?"

"We must first give you an alias, but only if you pledge an oath to *the cause*."

"The cause, sir?"

Sir Donald pointed to a silk rose on his lapel, one that Kier suspected served as a secret symbol used by the Jacobites.

Pledge an oath to an exiled king?

In a way, he'd already become a Jacobite *and* he'd already altered his name to Camp. Kier glanced down at the hopeful expression on his wife's face. "You once told me you wanted to see the Isle of Skye, love."

"Please," she tugged his arm. "We might even be able to see my family again."

Kier faced the baronet and gestured to the street. "Then lead on, Sir Donald. I would, indeed, be interested in your proposition."

Epilogue

30th September, 1695

More than three years had passed since the Glencoe Massacre. Kier, now living under the guise of Magnus Prince, overseer of a thriving salt pan operation, sat in his solar in Duntulm Castle overlooking the sea. News didn't oft come to Trotternish, but today he read through a two-month-old gazette dated 20th of June. After all this time, the Scottish Parliament had finally conducted an inquisition into the massacre. The Privy Council named the Master of Stair, Major Robert Duncanson, Captain Glenlyon, Lieutenant Lindsay and a handful of others as guilty of the slaughter of the Glencoe men under trust. No mention was made of Kier's guilt or innocence. He wasn't even named as one of the members of Glenlyon's regiment. Upon the writing of the article, no men had been summoned for prosecution and no reparations had been offered to Hugh and his crippled clan.

Kier set down the gazette and listened to the laughter of his daughter, Isabelle, as her wee voice echoed through the timbers above stairs. At the age of two, she had become quite a handful. And her newborn brother, Robert, was keeping his mother awake all hours.

After Isabelle had been born, Skye had boarded one of the salt transports bound for Glasgow and had taken the bairn to the Coe to see her family. Her parents had rebuilt their cottage and Tommy had grown so much, he was now taller than his sister.

Kier hoped that, with the outcome of the inquisition, he could clear his name and have his record of good service reinstated. Though he would never again don a red coat.

A quiet knock came at the door and his wife peeked her bonny head inside. "We have a visitor."

Standing, Kier chuckled. It wasn't often anyone ventured up the north shore of the Isle of Skye. Even the Baronet of Sleat had only made the journey twice in three years. "Do not keep me in suspense, Wife. Tell me who it is."

Grinning mischievously, she pushed the door open wide.

A lump formed in Kier's throat while his stomach squeezed. How in God's name had Da found him?

The old man stood in the passageway, his eyes rimmed red. He held up the same copy of the gazette as he shuffled into the solar. "Och, Son, I couldn't go to my grave without telling you how proud you have made me."

"I—"

"Allow me to finish." Da held up his palm. "I raised you to be an honorable man. I taught you to stand by your values, yet when the time came to take a stand against tyranny, I chose the wrong side. You, Son, chose the right. On that cold and frigid night three years past, the student became the teacher. I only pray God will see half the honor in me that I recognize in you. Can you ever forgive me?"

Tears welled in Kier's eyes as he pulled his father into his embrace for the first time since he was a bairn. "Och, Da, 'tis hard to turn your back on hundreds of years of clan fealty. I have always loved you as your son."

Through his blurry vision, he could see the tears dribbling from Skye's bonny blue eyes but her smile was more radiant than ever. She stepped in and placed her hand on Kier's shoulder. "This day is a gift from heaven for us all."

A Note from Amy Jarecki

Thank you for joining me for *The Highlander's Iron Will*. Though it's a short novella, I enjoyed going back to Glencoe after writing *The Fearless Highlander* (Hugh and Charlotte's story) and creating a fictional romance between Kier and Skye.

Usually, my main characters are developed after people who existed and I mold fiction to bring their histories to life. But for this story, Kier and Skye are both fictional characters as is Sigurd Castle on Loch Dochart. The horrific tragedy of Glencoe, however, will forever be a black mark in Scotland's history. Robert Campbell of Glenlyon did lead his regiment into the Coe, accept Clan Iain Abrach's hospitality for a fortnight, received orders from Major Duncanson and put them to fire and sword in the midst of a blizzard.

Robert Campbell, 5th Chieftain of Glenlyon, indeed, had a reputation for drinking and gambling his estate away and became the oldest captain in the king's army at the request of his earl cousins, Argyll and Breadalbane. As an officer, he received pay and work that his cousins hoped would keep Robert from their coffers. It is said that after the massacre, Glenlyon could be found in an Edinburgh alehouse, nursing a tankard as he sat against the wall in a dark corner with a haunted stare on his face. People would come to observe the spectacle of that crazed, aging man. "I would do it again!" he reportedly would holler. "I would dirk any man in Scotland or England without asking cause if the king gave me orders."

Some reports said, "MacIain hangs about Glenlyon day and night." Indeed, the man's soul was haunted.

The missive to Captain Campbell ordering the massacre was written by Major Robert Duncanson in Ballachulish on 12th February, 1692, and was said to have been passed down through Glenlyon's kin until it ended up in the possession of the National Library of Scotland in Edinburgh where it resides today. It reads:

You are hereby ordered to fall upon the Rebells, the M'Donalds of Glencoe, and putt all to the sword under seventy. You are to have a special care that the old fox and his sones do upon no account escape your hands. You are to secure all the avenues that no man escape. This you are to putt in execution ate five of the clock precisely and by that time, or verie shortly after it, I'le strive to be att you with a stronger party; if I doe not come to you at five, you are not to tarry for me, butt to fall on. This is by the King's special command, for the good and safety of the country, that these miscreanis be cut of root and branch. See that this be putt in executoine without feud or favour, else you may expect to be dealt with as one not true to King nor Government, not a man fit to carry commission in the King's Service. Expecting you will not faill in the ful-filling hereof, as you love yourselfe, I subscribe these with my hand at Balicholis, Ffeb. 12, 1692.

R. Duncanson
"To Capt. Robert Campbell of Glenlyon."
"ffor their Maties service."**

Interestingly, five o'clock was two hours before dawn, and Colonel Hill's original missive stated seven o'clock. That Major Duncanson wanted no part of the killing was clear, for when he did arrive with his battalion at seven that ill-fated morning, the killing had been done and the survivors were fleeing into the hills in the midst of a blizzard.

Though three years later, the Privy Council did conduct an inquisition and found the Master of Stair, Glenlyon, Duncanson and others guilty of murder under trust, John (Hugh) MacIain MacDonald and his clan never saw a penny of recompense. Further, though convicted, penalties were not enforced, and not one "murderer" spent a single minute behind bars.

Today, Glencoe is a thriving place of awe-inspiring landscape and is home to an abundance of wildlife. In the town of Glencoe there is a lovely museum displaying remnants of the early life. A memorial still stands giving ode to Alasdair MacIain MacDonald, the fearless old laird. Up the A82, the National Trust for Scotland has built an impressive visitors center with something for everyone. Glencoe truly is one of nature's grand fortresses, one well worth a visit.

Read more Highland Defender novels *or* Lords of the Highlands, as the series continues with Hachette Book Group's imprint, Forever:

The Fearless Highlander

Meet Hugh MacIain, heir to the most notorious clan in the Highlands

The Valiant Highlander

When the Baronet of Sleat faces musket-wielding Mary of Castleton, he's convinced they are utterly incompatible. But sometimes even a brawny Highlander can meet his match.

Brought to you by Hachette Book Group's Forever Imprint

The Highland Duke

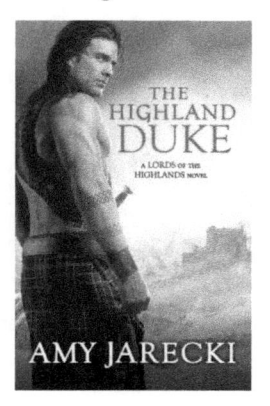

She will put her life on the line for him. Yet she can never know his true identity.

The Highland Commander

She cannot resist the man behind the mask.

The Highland Guardian

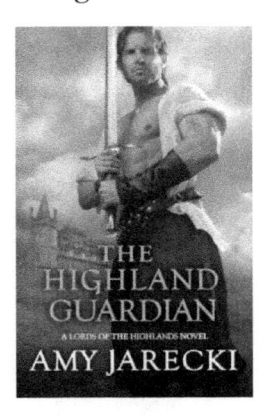

He has sworn to protect her, but he might be her greatest threat.

Other Books by Amy Jarecki:

Visit http://amyjarecki.com/books or your retailer for links:

Highland Defender/Lords of the Highlands Series:

The Fearless Highlander
The Valiant Highlander
The Highland Duke
The Highland Commander
The Highland Guardian (Preorder for Dec. 2019 Release)
The Highland Chieftain (July, 2018)

Guardian of Scotland Time Travel Series
Rise of a Legend
In the Kingdom's Name
The Time Traveler's Christmas

Highland Dynasty Series:
Knight in Highland Armor
A Highland Knight's Desire
A Highland Knight to Remember
Highland Knight of Rapture

Highland Force Series:
Captured by the Pirate Laird
The Highland Henchman
Beauty and the Barbarian
Return of the Highland Laird (A Highland Force Novella)

Pict/Roman Romances:
Rescued by the Celtic Warrior

Celtic Maid

Do not miss ICE, Amy's latest Romantic Suspense series!
Hunt for Evil
Body Shot
Mach One (January 2, 2018)

Visit http://amyjarecki.com/books or your retailer for links:

If you enjoyed *The Highlander's Iron Will* we would be honored if you would consider leaving a review. *~Thank you!*

About the Author

Amy embarked on her writing journey shortly after she completed an MBA with Heriot-Watt University in Edinburgh, Scotland. Her first manuscripts were suspense novels and were never published. She calls them baptism by fire—lessons in learning to write fiction. These lessons, combined with several writing conferences and classes, led her to write her first published book, *Boy Man Chief*, which won the League of Utah Writers award for Best Manuscript, and the Spark Book Award.

A lot has happened since, with some of the highlights being *Rise of a Legend* winning the RONE award for Best Time Travel; hitting the Amazon Top 100 Bestseller list; and a host of other accolades.

Amy enjoys the freedom of authorship and the opportunity to work creatively every day. She has lived in Australia, Bermuda and has spent extensive time in Scotland. Whenever possible, she visits the places she writes about to add vibrant realism to her stories.

She loves writing Scottish historical romance, and now she's adding romantic suspense to the mix. Come along for the ride!

Amy loves hearing from her readers and can be contacted through her website at http://amyjarecki.com/.

Visit Amy's website & sign up to receive newsletter updates of new releases and giveaways exclusive to newsletter followers.

CPSIA information can be obtained
at www.ICGtesting.com
Printed in the USA
BVHW03s1151130918
527438BV00001B/10/P